NEGOTIATING POINT

PRIVATE PROTECTORS SERIES

ADRIENNE GIORDANO

ALG PUBLISHING

Edited by Gina Bernal

Copyedited by Elizabeth Neal

Cover Design by Lewellen Designs

Author Photo by Debora Giordano

Print Edition ISBN: 978-1-942504-61-0

Digital Edition ISBN: 978-1-942504-60-3

1
———

At ten-twenty, Gavin stepped into Mike Taylor's office and found his boss sitting at his pristine, glass-topped desk, his sleeves rolled to his elbows and his dark hair sticking up in the back.

He checked his watch. Yep. Ten-twenty.

I'm screwed.

The man's appearance was typically as neat as his office. His hair sticking up? This early? In Mike's OCD world? Unacceptable.

Whatever Gavin had been summoned for had to be a disaster. Stabbing pin pricks crawled up his neck. He shifted his gaze left. Vic Andrews, Taylor Security's executive vice president, leaned against the windowsill with his arms crossed, eyes narrowed and a general I'm-pissed-off-at-the-world aura.

Screwed.

Gavin stepped forward. "What's up?"

Mike held his hands prayerlike in front of him, his fingers mashed together until his veins popped.

Screwed in a big way.

Vic boosted off the windowsill. "Roxann has been kidnapped."

Bam! Forget the warm-up. Gavin threw his shoulders back and those pin pricks turned to dagger stabs. Had he heard right? He shifted to Mike. "Your Roxann?"

Mike nodded.

"Have they made contact? Ransom?"

"Not yet. I got a call a few minutes ago. They said no cops and to expect communication in the next hour."

"Where'd they grab her?"

Mike looked down, shook his head and scrubbed his hands over his face. "I don't know. We left together this morning. She was heading to the lake house to get ready for the Fourth of July party on Saturday. I've got Gizmo tracing her car."

That wouldn't do them any good. Even the most inexperienced kidnapper would know a high-end Mercedes would have factory-installed tracking. Couple that with the car being owned by the man who ran not only Chicago's, but one of the nation's most elite private security companies and it was a no-brainer they'd be able to locate the car. The kidnappers probably abandoned it somewhere. Mike knew that and Gavin wouldn't voice it.

"Are you considering calling the FBI?"

Vic moved to the side of the desk. "No feds."

Gavin ignored him. "Mike?"

"No FBI."

Lost that round.

"The FBI," Mike continued, "has to play by the rules. We don't. I want my wife back without having to deal with red tape."

"Damn straight," Vic added. "We got everything we need. We find her and we get her. End of story."

Gavin finally looked at him. "End of story? What's wrong with you? You and your merry men charging in there with your flash bangs and weapons will escalate the situation."

"Screw that," Vic said. "These assholes won't know what hit them. Once we find her, we'll be in there so fast they won't have time to draw on us. Besides, what the hell do we need the FBI for when we have you?"

Gavin breathed deep. A sound argument considering, prior to six months ago, he'd spent the last twelve years as an FBI hostage negotiator. "Has it occurred to you that we are not in some war-torn country? You're talking about a takedown on U.S. soil. In case you weren't aware, if someone gets shot, there are laws against that sort of thing."

Mike put both hands up. "Enough." He dragged his gaze from Vic to Gavin. "Look, Gavin, all due respect, I'm not calling the feds."

"Thank you," Vic said.

"But we're not going tactical either. *Yet.* Gavin will negotiate her release."

There it was. The assignment of his career.

"Mike," Vic said, "why waste time trying to head-shrink our way out of this?"

Jab number one. Gavin folded his arms, let the anger inside flash and burn before reacting. Considering Vic was married to Mike's sister and his own emotions were likely in play, he'd give him a pass on the head-shrinker comment. "We're not *head-shrinking.* We don't know who these people are or what they want. Let's figure that out and then make a plan."

A ding sounded from Mike's email. He spun to the laptop, shook the mouse and stared at the screen. The muscle in his jaw throbbed. "Here it is."

Gavin swung around the desk to read over Mike's shoulder. Within the email was a link. No message. Mike clicked the link before Gavin could warn him about possible computer viruses. Not a top priority when the man's wife had been kidnapped.

A video popped on the screen and Roxann's classically beautiful face—the blue eyes, the perfect cheekbones, the blond hair, appeared. The background was a white wall, no markings or hanging artwork. No intel there.

Before clicking the play arrow, Mike blew out a heaving breath that sounded like it had stripped him raw. Probably had.

Gavin touched his shoulder. "Let me do this. Take a walk or something."

Mike shook him off, clicked the button and they watched Roxann glance beyond the camera. "Now?" she said.

True to her legendary control—or maybe it was her experience with running a major market newspaper—her voice stayed steady and direct. Roxann Taylor might be a rock star when it came to putting on a brave face, but he'd spent last weekend with this couple. He'd seen her relax and banter with her husband over his goading, teasing comments. The stoic person on this video was indicative of Roxann Taylor the controlled executive. Not Roxann Taylor the loving wife.

That alone ripped into Gavin and his chest ached for the man sitting in front of him.

Someone must have signaled Roxann because she looked down, her blond hair falling in front of her face as she read from notes. The video had a grainy quality to it. Cell phone. Had to be.

"My captors are part of the Freedom Today group. Their leader, the most-esteemed Jackson Spelling, is wrongly incarcerated for plotting to murder a judge. Mr. Spelling is innocent and the Freedom Today group demands his release. Further, the group expects my husband to use his government contacts to help with Mr. Spelling's release. The group also demands that my newspaper run a front-page story on Mr. Spelling's wrongful conviction. You will be contacted again at noon today with instructions."

The screen went black. A breath-stealing silence hung heavy in the room; the energy shot through with nervous tension. "Play it again."

Vic waved a hand, the white of his dress shirt flashing in Gavin's peripheral vision. "Mike, go for a walk. We'll deal with this."

"I'm fine."

But he didn't move and they continued to stare at him, waiting for him to play the video. Mike's gaze locked on a solid crystal paperweight that could split someone's head.

Gavin reached for the rounded crystal which, indeed, packed some heft and handed it to his boss, who glanced up at him, his eyes hard. *Yes, I've head-shrinked you.* "Go for it. Let loose so you can focus."

With that, Mike jumped out of his chair and launched the paperweight against the wall with the force of a ninety-mile-per-hour fastball. Upon its booming impact, the paperweight shattered, spraying shards of pulverized glass over the sofa and floor. Helluva mess there. "Better?"

Mike sucked in air, held it a minute and let it go. "Yes."

"Good. Play that video again."

Mike clicked the button and the video started. Nothing. No car horns. No television or radio in the background. Just Roxann and a drab off-white wall.

"Okay," Gavin said. "Can I bring Janet in on this?"

Janet Fink. Resident tech geek. The woman could do things with computers that nearly gave him an orgasm.

"Of course," Mike said. "We'll use every asset we have."

Gavin reached for the desk phone and dialed.

"Hi, Michael," Janet said.

"It's Gavin. In Mike's office. Can you get here ASAP?"

"On my way."

Two minutes later she rushed through the door, her hesitant gaze blazing around the room to the three of them. *Welcome to the nightmare.* She must have sprinted up the two flights of stairs, but her shoulder-length honey-blond hair remained secure in a hair clip. The look only accentuated her softly rounded face and big brown eyes. She wore a sleeveless blouse and snug-fitting pants that emphasized her petite frame. The woman couldn't be more than 105 pounds.

Avoiding his gaze, she turned to Mike still sitting at his desk. "What's happening?"

Gavin took that one. "We have a situation. Roxann has been kidnapped."

Janet's dark eyes finally shifted to him. *"Kidnapped?"*

No one answered. She accepted the silence as affirmation and faced Mike. "My God. I'm so sorry. What can I do?"

Gavin waved her behind the desk. "Take a look at this video. I think they used a cell phone. Can you get me the number and location?"

She slid around the desk and Mike signaled her to his chair. "Watch the whole thing. We're gonna need you to work your contacts for info on this group."

"While she's doing that," Gavin said, "how do you want to handle the request about the story in the *Banner?*"

Mike shook his head. "Roxi would never go for that."

"Not a chance." This from Vic. "She won't be bullied into a story."

"Do the executives at the *Banner* know about this?" Gavin asked.

"Only her secretary. Rox was supposed to stop at the office on the way to the lake. When she didn't show, Mrs. Mackey called me. I had to tell her."

Vic straightened. "Let's wait for the call and tell them we're sending a reporter. We'll send one of our guys in. He can report back and we move. Done deal."

Again with going tactical. *Pain in the ass.*

"No," Gavin said. "You want to send one of your guys in, fine. I can use the intel for negotiations."

"Listen, head-shrinker." Vic jabbed his finger. "I'm not dicking around with you. We need to get her out of there."

Yeah, hello. The head-shrinker thing was starting to piss him off. That would be a fight for later though. "I'm not risking her getting hurt when you knuckle-draggers bust in there and cause panic. We have no idea what we're dealing with. We don't know what kind of weapons they have or if they're capable of using them. Let me get information first."

If the knuckle-dragger comment had even dented Vic's buzz-cut blond head, it didn't show. Mike once again held his hands to them. "Gavin is right. We need information. Let's get that and decide on a plan."

"Mike!" Vic hollered.

Mike spun on him and, despite being a few inches shorter than Vic, he had a way of getting large with people. "We're doing it Gavin's way. She's pregnant. I can't take a chance."

And, whoa, everyone stopped moving. Including maybe Gavin's heart.

"Holy shit," Vic said.

Mike puffed out his cheeks and blew air. "I didn't want to tell you that way. I found out this morning. We wanted to tell everyone this weekend."

JANET'S FINGERS TREMBLED AS THEY FLEW OVER THE keyboard. What did one say to a man who found out he would be a father on the same day of his wife's kidnapping?

Congratulations?

I'm sorry?

No idea. But she could keep working this video and hope the owner didn't turn off the phone's geotagging function. Geotags would tell them where the video was shot and that was what she needed.

"Jesus, Mike," Vic said.

Janet glanced up at him, hoping he wouldn't be his typical free-wheeling self and mouth off. She went back to the screen in front of her. *Come to Mama.* "Got it!"

"Where?" Vic said.

"Keep your shorts on, boss, and I'll get an address." She went to a map, typed in the long and lat. "Denson, Illinois. By Kankakee. Major farm country there." She jotted the address.

Vic snatched the paper from her. "I'll check it out."

"Let's not do anything stupid," Mike said. "I'd go with you but the next call will come soon."

"I'm good. If I can verify she's there, we'll know where to start and head-shrinker here can do his thing."

Janet sighed. "You know, that head-shrinker thing is just rude."

His response was an out-of-character—at least when it came to her—glare and she curled her toes inside her ballet slipper shoes.

"Take it easy, girlfriend. We're all on the same team. Besides, he can take it."

With that, Vic walked out leaving Michael shaking his head. "Gavin—"

"Forget it, Mike. Bigger things to mess with here. Vic and I will work it out. Eventually. Janet, if we confirm her location, we'll set up a command post and you'll need to get us wired."

"No problem. I'll head downstairs and get what we'll need. I'll make calls, see who knows what about this Freedom Today group. If they're a major player, my contacts at the CIA will have them on a list somewhere."

AN HOUR LATER, WITH VIC ON SPEAKERPHONE, GAVIN STOOD next to Mike's desk counting down the eighteen minutes until their next communication from the kidnappers. Janet sat in one of the leather guest chairs, notepad in hand.

"What have you got?" Mike asked Vic.

"It's a farmhouse. There's a car parked in the driveway. No activity outside. Shades are pulled. I got a plate number for the car. And relax, head-shrinker, I didn't go near the house."

Pain in the ass. "So, no way to tell if Roxann is inside?"

"No."

Janet raised her hand to get their attention. "When they call, let's have Mike ask to speak to Rox, then I can get a location for the phone. If the address is a match for the farmhouse, we know that's where she is."

"Beautiful," Vic said.

Love this woman. Maybe they'd get Roxann and her unborn baby released unharmed. "Vic, check the area for somewhere to set up a command post."

"On it."

"We'll keep you posted." Mike disconnected, ran his hands over his face and sat back. "Now we wait?"

Gavin nodded. "Now we wait." He turned to Janet. "How confident are you that you can grab the phone's location?"

She glanced at Mike, then back to Gavin. "In my downtime, I've hacked into the top three cell carrier's systems. If the phone is part of one of their networks, I can get its location. I retrieved the number from when they sent the video. All I'd have to do this time is check the location of the phone they're talking on and make sure it matches."

"I love you," Mike said.

She shrugged. "I'm a geek who likes a challenge. I thought having access to cell carrier networks would come in handy at some point. If they use a different phone, I'll have to get that number."

Mike's cell rang and he scooped it up. "Blocked number."

They're early. Interesting.

Leaping from her chair, Janet shooed Mike from his spot near the computer. Quick little woman, that one.

"If it's them," Gavin said to Mike, "don't agree to anything. Fact finding here."

Mike hit the speaker button. "Michael Taylor."

"This is Joe Smith from Freedom Today. If you meet our demands, your wife will be returned unharmed."

"Put her on."

"No."

"I'm not agreeing to any demands until I know she's okay."

Muffled voices came through the speaker. Joe Smith probably put his hand over the phone. *More than one captor.*

And Joe Smith? Could he have picked a better fake name? Totally generic.

More muffled sounds filled the otherwise silent office and Mike tapped his fingers against the edge of his desk. For some reason, Gavin thought of the fingerprints that would be left on the glass. He supposed it was easier than staring at Mike who waited for the sound of his pregnant wife's voice.

Gavin breathed in when his mind flashed to his mother crying herself to sleep after his dad had died. As he'd done many times, he stored the bits of memory, one by one, into his brain's hideaways.

The muffling noise from the other end of the phone disappeared. A beep sounded. Speakerphone. "Hi," Roxann said in her steady, control-freak voice.

Mike straightened, closed his eyes for a second and dropped his head to his chest. In that moment, Gavin imagined a bizarre combination of grief and respite pressing his boss further and further into turmoil.

"Are you hurt?" Mike asked his wife.

"No. I'm okay."

"That's enough." Male voice—*Joe Smith.* "Now you've spoken to her. She is unharmed and if you want her to stay that way, her newspaper will run an article we've prepared. Tomorrow's paper. It will be emailed to your account. By 5:00 p.m. By the end of the day tomorrow, we want Jackson Spelling released from prison."

Gavin rolled his hand for Mike to keep talking. Any new info would help.

"Look," Mike said, but the line went dead.

He squeezed the phone, his fingers straining against it before he ran his thumb over the screen. Along with the connection, his link to Roxann had been severed and it left Gavin with a gut-burn that might tear a hole in him.

Just get her back.

"She's okay," Gavin said. "And we've already got a lead on her location. They'll call again when the email is sent. They'll confirm you got it."

"Right." Mike set the phone on the desk with precision care, his gaze not leaving it.

Horrible fucking pressure.

"Got it!" Janet yelled and they both swiveled to see her face lit with her never-ending energy. "It's the same location as before. That's where they have her."

Mike bent over, straddled his hands over his thighs and stared at the floor. He glanced back to Janet. "Whatever I'm paying you, you're getting a raise."

Then he marched out of the room.

FEELING THE ELECTRIC WHOOSH OF HER SUCCESS, JANET jumped from the chair, reached across the desk and high-fived Gavin. Their hands connected and he wrapped his fingers around hers, sending her filthy mind back to the blazing kiss they'd shared three weeks earlier after working a kidnap and ransom case.

At thirty-two she remained the lone woman on the team and, as such, worked hard to ensure the burly, manly men saw her as an essential asset rather than a woman who happened to be there for their amusement. At least until Mr. Sexy Galore Gavin Sheppard came aboard. James Bond may have had Pussy Galore, but Janet Fink had Sexy Galore. This man, with his dark hair and eyes, could make a smart girl turn stupid.

Fast.

Be a smart girl.

Maybe that hand squeeze was just a friendly thing. Sort

of an I-don't-want-to-do-you-but-you-did-good squeeze. Yes, that was it. She'd done her job well. Something she always strived for.

But then he pinned those sultry brown eyes on her and she started to rethink the idea that maybe he *did* want to do her. Touching him had been an epic mistake. According to her brain anyway. Her body had differing opinions. After another paralyzing second of heat pouring from his hand, he let go.

Double darn. Heaven help her, she didn't know what she wanted. *Touch me, don't touch me. Touch me, don't touch me.* This was what she should have experienced in high school when everyone's hormones but hers bugged out. Back then she found solace hiding behind her computer because the short, bean-pole geek would rather talk code than boys. The girls thought her weird and the boys found little appreciation for her A-cup breasts. Pretty much, everyone ignored her.

"Thank you," he said.

She rubbed her hands together to replace the warmth that had abandoned her. "We'll get her back. I know we will."

I just have to keep my hands off you until we do.

2

____

In the abandoned barn Vic had located adjacent to the kidnapper's location, Janet plugged the last cord into a video screen and pressed the button. The cameras being placed in various locations would feed them images of the house.

The screen blinked and the front of the kidnappers' house appeared.

She moved to the next task of powering up the remaining monitors while scanning the available space. The barn sat on twelve acres of bank-owned farmland for sale. A shame for the owners, but for today, Taylor Security appreciated the use of the open two-story structure. She drew a breath of hot, stale air.

They'd have to leave the door cracked to air the place out.

Not wanting to risk any police officers checking up on them, they'd made sure to park their cars behind the barn and out of sight from the road. All they needed was a sheriff traipsing in and seeing a full command center.

Janet took a minute to survey the folding tables covered

with electronic equipment and, given her time restraints, considered her handiwork a job well-done. Generators were such a lovely invention. How she love, love, loved her job.

They'd even brought in a cot in case they were here for days and needed naps. She knew from the South America trip Gavin could work on minimal sleep, but he didn't pretend to be Superman. He knew when his body needed rest. Another thing she admired about him. Some of the guys on the team pushed themselves to the brink to prove they were the biggest and baddest. Gavin didn't bother. He knew his worth. Seriously, could there be anything hotter than a man comfortable with himself?

A trickle of sweat dripped down the side of her face and she swiped at it.

Sexy Galore didn't seem to be sweating. In this heat, how could that be? The short-sleeved golf shirt he'd changed into didn't have one ring of sweat. Anywhere. Meanwhile she looked like she'd just run thirty miles.

Vic strode through the open barn door. "Hey, head-shrinker."

"Hey, knuckle-dragger," Gavin shot back and Janet's knees crumbled more than a little because—*wow*—the man just, for the *second* time, called one of the toughest guys on earth a knuckle-dragger.

Sexy.

Galore.

"Nice." Vic gave a half grin. "Your cell phone issue is taken care of."

"Signal jammer?"

"No. It's something Gizmo has been working on. The device blocks anything outgoing. If necessary, we can tweak it so all calls go straight to voicemail. The hostage takers can retrieve voice mails and that's it. They won't be able to figure out why their phones aren't ringing."

"I love Gizmo," Janet said. "The phone still works so we're not breaking any laws by jamming the signal."

"You got it, sister."

Gavin nodded. "Have your team ready in case I need them."

"On it." He glanced around at the equipment. "Where are we?"

Janet held her hand high. Being the shrimp she was, sometimes it was the only way to get anyone's attention. "I just confirmed the land line has been shut off. The house is owned by a Madeline Burger. Well, it was owned by her. She died three weeks ago."

"Whoa," Vic said.

"No idea how these people came to be squatting in this dead woman's house but I'm working on it. Turns out Freedom Today has a Facebook page. They're some kind of political group, but I can't get a handle on what exactly their platform is. As soon as I get in there, I might be able to see who the members are and find someone with the last name Burger. Anyway, the land line for the phone was shut off by..." she checked her notes, "...Collin Burger. According to the guy at the phone company, Collin is Madeline's son."

"And you got this information how?" Gavin asked.

"We provide security for the phone company's corporate headquarters. Mike called the CEO and did his thing."

Gavin smiled. "I love how you people work."

Sexy Galore must still be adjusting to civilian life. In his FBI world, warrants were everything. Without a warrant or with a minor language issue on a warrant, the whole case could be blown to bits. One tiny piece of evidence collected outside the scope of a warrant could make—or break—a case.

Vic's team didn't worry about warrants.

They didn't have to.

Gavin turned to Vic. "I'm about to call one Joe Smith and see if he'll talk to me. Did you set up my perimeter?"

Vic jerked his head. "You got a three-sixty. My guys are out of sight, but nobody leaves or enters that property without us knowing."

"Good. Tell your men to stand down. No firing. Let me initiate contact and see if they'll talk to me. Clear?"

If at all possible, the air in the barn compressed and became more stifling. Janet eased out a breath. Leaves rustled in the wind outside the open door, but somehow it intensified the searing friction bouncing off the two men in front of her. Michael may have been the one to woo her from the CIA four years ago, but she'd been part of Vic's elite team of spec ops guys since the day she had walked through the door. She knew him well enough to know he was about to lose his patience.

Vic stepped closer, got right into Gavin's face, and her feet glued themselves to the floor. Not that she—with her diminutive stature—would be able to get between them, but still, to be rendered immobile? She dragged her gaze from Gavin to Vic and back while a tingling buzz flicked at her skin. Was it a sick thing that she found this mildly intoxicating?

Vic stood a good five inches taller than Gavin, but Sexy Galore took no garbage from him. Rather than trying to bulk up to compete with the guys on the team, Gavin had dropped weight since coming to Taylor Security. She liked his coiled muscles opposed to the hulking, beefed-up look most of the guys on the team went for.

Of course, she spent far too much time studying Gavin's physique from far too many angles.

Feel that, Janet? It's a smart girl turning stupid.

"Yeah, we're clear," Vic said. "But if I think your therapy session is crashing, we're going tactical. *Clear?*"

Michael entered the barn, saw the two men toe-to-toe and shook his head. "What the hell is this?"

"Nothing," Vic said. "We're setting ground rules."

"What's your hurry?" Gavin asked, his eyes still on Vic. "You can always kill these guys tomorrow."

Game on. Movement in her limbs returned and Janet shot her hands toward the ceiling. They'd destroy each other if this kept up. "Stop! Everybody take a breath."

But Michael charged over to where they stood. "This pissing match ends now." He turned to Vic. "You want ground rules. Gavin gets until nightfall to talk these assholes down. My pregnant wife is in that house and you wanna bust in there with automatic weapons? I don't think so. Too risky. We've contained them, we've limited their phone use and we know Roxann is doing reasonably well. For now, this is Gavin's show. If he can initiate contact and talk these whack-jobs into letting my wife go, we'll call it a good day. A fucking excellent day. Until then, you offer support when necessary. By nightfall, if there's no movement, we'll revisit going tactical. Until then, everybody shuts up. Am *I* clear?"

Without moving an inch, Gavin said, "I'm good."

Vic spun on his booted feet and stormed toward the door. "Roger that."

Michael watched him go, shook his head and turned to Janet. "What do we know about this group?"

"My CIA guy doesn't have anything on them. They seem to be grass-roots. No history of violence."

"Which is good," Gavin added.

Michael nodded. "Right. Are you ready to make contact?"

"Yes."

"I'll do my best to stay out of here. I need you focused and I don't want my emotions in the way. There's a truck stop down the road. I'll squat there, but you need to keep me updated. Often."

They waited for Michael to leave the barn. Janet started to speak, but Gavin held his hand up. When a car door slammed, he turned back to her. "I wanted him out of earshot. Do we know anything about Joe Smith? Any priors? Anything?"

Janet shifted to her laptop. "*His* Facebook page I've already gotten into."

"I guess these people like Facebook."

"They do. Social media is the bomb when it comes to spreading your message. And, believe it or not, Joe Smith is his real name."

"Fantastic. Leave it to me to get a guy with an unbelievably common name. It'll take a year to gather intel on him."

"So, *anyway,* Mr. Negative, I was able to grab his birthday from his account. I don't know why people insist on putting the year there. It makes it so much easier for hackers."

"Uh, hello? Facebook?"

"Right. Sorry. I asked a friend at the PD to run a check on his name and birthday. Assuming the birthday he listed is the actual, there were no matches for our Joe Smith. No criminal history. We know he was on the chess team in high school, went to USC and was a math major. He's just a general geek."

Gavin leaned back on the makeshift desk. "In other words, he seems like a straight-up guy. So what happened?

How the hell did he get mixed up with this group and kidnap a publisher?"

She knew exactly what happened. Geeks understood other geeks. Her guess was he wanted to fit in somewhere. "He probably wanted to be part of something. Maybe he's a little vulnerable and met someone who followed this group. This group took one look at Joe Smith and saw a malleable person desperate for friends."

Gavin tilted his head, considered it. "Okay. I'll go with that."

She stared at her notepad, flicked her finger against it. "Us geeks, we want to be part of something that feels like it matters. To belong."

And, oh, my God. Did she really cough up that hairball? Pathetic, lonely elf misunderstood by all. Swallowing the humiliation, she met Gavin's gaze.

He twisted his lips and tilted his head for a second. Studying her. As a former FBI hostage negotiator with a master's degree in psychology, he knew how to actively listen and study people's habits. That's what good negotiators did—they watched, they listened, they stayed calm.

Don't you dare shrink my head, Sexy.

"What you're telling me, is I can connect with him on the wanting-to-belong angle."

Yes, Sexy Galore, you are a brilliant man for not making me feel like a freak. "That's exactly what I'm saying. The way to get inside this guy's head is to make him think you understand what it's like to be an outcast due to his brainiac status."

Gavin jotted notes. "I can do that. Does he have any hang-ups? Hates swearing? A religious zealot? Anything?"

"Nothing on that yet. I can go through his updates on Facebook and see if there are any hot buttons."

"Good. Let's roll. You ready?"

She spun to her laptop; fingers poised. "Ready."

GAVIN DIALED THE NUMBER JANET HAD PROVIDED FOR JOE Smith and waited to see how this opening volley would go. More than likely, Joe would nearly soil himself when he realized who was on the other end of the line. After said soiling, Joe would hang up.

"Hello?" came a man's voice.

"Joe?" Gavin asked, sounding like the guy's best friend.

"Yeah. Who's this?"

"This is Gavin Sheppard. I work for Taylor Security—"

Click. Gavin sighed—*let's play ball*—and redialed. He turned to Janet. "He hung up."

"Of course he did."

The phone rang again, but went to voice mail. "He cannot believe I'm going away. Can he?"

Gavin settled into the folding chair behind him and hit Redial. Dipshit Joe Smith didn't know Gavin had the tenacity to sit here all day dialing this number. He wouldn't do that though. Soon, he'd do that tweak Vic mentioned and disable Joe's cell. Then they'd deliver a throw phone, a dedicated line allowing the kidnappers to speak only with him.

He'd spend a week talking a hostage taker down if it avoided tactical assault. Vic was the tactical guy, always ready to take up arms. In the six months of Gavin's employ at Taylor Security, he and Vic hadn't yet figured out how to merge their expertise and play nice. Gavin didn't necessarily have a problem going tactical, but it meant all other attempts to resolve the situation had failed.

Gavin didn't like to fail.

Going tactical also carried the highest risk of someone getting hurt. Or killed. In this case, that someone could be Roxann Taylor.

He redialed. Nothing.

Gavin stood, slipped a headset on, walked across the width of the barn to the rectangular table where he found the case containing the throw phone. He grabbed it and the bullhorn sitting next to it. "I'll be back. Hopefully."

And when had he become so warped that he could be sarcastic about this? Probably after the hostage situation in Arkansas ten months ago. That fiasco wasn't his fuck-up but he was one of four FBI negotiators assigned to it.

The twelve dead people, all members of a cult murdered by their leader, were his motivating factor for leaving the Bureau after twelve years. At thirty-eight years old, he'd been aging fast in a job that was bleeding the life out of him.

Enter Mike Taylor and his ridiculously appealing offer.

"Be careful," Janet called after him.

"I'll use the guys to cover me. They'll do that stacking thing they love with the shields and I'll throw the phone through a window."

Janet jumped from her chair. "Hang on. You need a vest and helmet."

She grabbed a vest from the box on the floor and held it up for him. He propped the bullhorn under the arm where he held the throw phone and slid his free arm into the tac vest.

"Now the other arm," she said.

"Yes, Mommy."

She laughed. "Come to Mama, sweetheart."

Maybe she was kidding, but dammit if that loop in his head of all the things he'd like to do to her didn't start spinning out of control. Visions of her under him, *naked,* whispering those same words, flashed. *Jeez, I'm a pervert.* He had to stop that loop. No matter how he sliced it—and he'd sliced it plenty—she was a support person. Maybe he wasn't her supervisor, but he held a senior position in this company and wasn't about to become the clichéd skirt-chasing executive. Right now, he had to find a way to bury, to *drown,* his personal feelings. The memory of that kiss three weeks ago needed to drown with it.

Making matters worse, he had an erection and needed to get the hell out of the barn before she spotted it. He'd just hold the bullhorn in front of his crotch to hide the traitor known as his wanger.

With his back still to her, he transferred the phone and bullhorn to his other side and slid his free arm into the vest. Then she planted a helmet on him, swung around to face him and went to work on the helmet's strap. Her fingertips brushed the underside of his chin, that slight touch kicking off a wicked buzzing under his skin.

He lowered the bullhorn.

"You're all set." She patted his face.

He stepped out of her reach because, yes, even her friendly touch made him crazy. No touching anymore. The temptation was too great and he couldn't risk it. For either one of them.

"You okay?" she asked.

He blinked a few times, trying to rid himself of that naked vision of her. "I'm—uh—confused."

"Confused?"

"*Conflicted* might be a better word. There's this...*thing...* between us."

"The smoking hot kiss you mean? *That* thing?"

He let out a short laugh, grateful for the levity she

always brought to a situation. "Yes. *That* thing. Now isn't the time, but we need to figure out what to do with it."

She reached to secure the strap on his vest, her gaze focused on the task. It would have been so, so easy to dip his head low and kiss her. Just feast on those lips for a while.

"I know what I'd like to do with it. And that's saying something because I have an iron-clad rule about not getting involved with coworkers."

"Yes," Gavin said. "There's the work issue. Technically, I'm an executive. You're not. I'm worried about the perception."

"As am I. So, we agree on that."

"Yes."

"Doesn't make it any easier though. Go deliver that phone. I'll see you when you get back."

He made his way out of the barn, passed Vic on the phone in his SUV and marched up the quiet country road where the only house to be seen was the one holding Roxann Taylor. He took a moment to center himself, to allow the warmth of the midday sun to soak him and imagined the pregnant Roxann Taylor walking out of this mess.

Not for one second would he allow the idea of her not being freed to enter his mind. Even when he'd have doubts, he'd keep them to himself. If any member of the team felt that doubt, they were done. One little seed could destroy an entire operation.

He reached the far end of the property and huddled behind a tree. Scanning the area, he knew Vic's alpha team was out here somewhere, but they were hidden well. Good news in case a patrol car went by. The cornfields in the back and on either side of the property could easily hide a man. If they had to have a barricade situation, this probably wasn't the worst place it could happen. The front of the property though didn't offer much cover and Gavin wondered where the hell those boys had buried themselves.

Still huddled behind the tree in case anyone decided to take a shot at him from the house, he pressed the button on the bullhorn.

"Joe, this is Gavin Sheppard. We have disabled your phones. I'm delivering a phone that will allow you to communicate with us. We're approaching the house only to deliver the phone. I'll throw it through the front window so you won't have to come out."

A huge black Taylor Security SUV pulled up. Five guys dressed in full riot gear and carrying shields jumped out. All they had to do was hope a copper didn't appear. That would be fun to explain. *You see, Officer, my boss's wife has been kidnapped and we figured law enforcement would screw it up.*

Goatfuck.

With that, he took a breath, prayed this wouldn't be his last voyage and stepped from behind the tree to the cover of Vic's team and their shields. One of the men pulled a shield from the truck for him and they lined up one behind each other with Gavin in the middle. In this stacked position, shields providing protection and the steady beat of Gavin's heart drowning all sounds inside his head, he found himself fully alert, but not panicked. When they reached the front of the house, Jessup jammed the break and rake tool through the window. Glass shattered, disrupting the quiet country air, and voices from inside streamed through the broken glass as Jessup tore the window blind out with the tool. Gavin held the shield in front of him in case some nut decided to shoot. With his free hand, he tossed the throw phone through the window.

Gavin hustled back to the stack of men and they

retreated, unwinding the cord connecting the phones as they went along.

WHEN GAVIN STEPPED INTO THE BARN A WAVE OF RELIEF consumed Janet. That had been a lifetime of a fifteen minutes. She'd been watching the action on the monitors to ensure Gavin's safety, but the tension that came with his absence had nearly paralyzed her.

She rose from her chair, walked to him and held her hand for a high-five. Unlike the last time they'd engaged in this celebratory habit, there was no prolonged touching and that suited her fine.

She thought. No. She knew. After all, she'd once been involved with another member of Vic's team and that hadn't turned out so well. The sexual tension between them sizzled but intellectually, they were a dead loss.

Dead loss.

But, oh, how the gossip mongers had their way with her. Never again would she allow herself to be fodder for the business office's witch twins, two women who spent every available minute battling for attention from the operatives. When word had gotten out about Janet and Duck, the twins wasted no time spreading vile nastiness about Janet sleeping her way into her job.

"Did it go okay?"

"Yeah," he said. "Let's see if they pick up."

He unloaded the bullhorn, shucked the helmet and vest and punched the button on his end of the two-way phone.

No answer.

What she learned about Gavin on their last assignment was he'd keep trying. The man never gave up and never gave in. How he handled the stress and the responsibility, she couldn't fathom, but this was a man dedicated to a nonviolent ending.

As difficult as these situations were, she found herself suited to the activity. To the challenge of it. Most of her work for Vic's team happened behind the scenes. Sure, she was integral and probably saved their asses on many occasions, but this...this *function* gave her the ability to literally save someone's life with the information she provided.

And that was a rush.

On a purely emotional level, she could see why Gavin had built a career on hostage negotiating. Saving a life was hero material. But losing a life, well, she didn't want to percolate on that aspect of his job.

She watched him fiddle with his headset before putting it on. "Why do you do this?"

"Beats the hell out of me."

"Seriously? You don't know?"

He punched the button on the phone again and waited. No answer. "I knew from the time I was a kid I wanted to work for the FBI. The dad of one of my friends worked for the Bureau and, after my own dad died, I latched on to the guy."

A lump settled in Janet's chest. "Your dad died when you were young?"

He tried the phone again. Waited. Nothing.

"I was thirteen and suddenly man of the house. The FBI dad was good to me. Used to take me fishing with them. He taught me a lot."

"Gosh, that had to be tough."

He finally turned to her. "It was tough on my mom. My dad had been the one to toss a baseball with me or play street hockey. She enjoyed sitting on the porch with her lemonade and watching. That life disappeared. I don't think she ever recovered."

"I'm so sorry. Did she ever remarry?"

He went back to the phone and tried again. Waited. Nothing. "Nope. She says my father was irreplaceable and she doesn't see any point in trying." He smiled and looked back at her, the features of his face softening. "I have to imagine she's been lonely all these years. Hell, my wife divorced me ten years ago and there are still times I miss having someone there when I get home. That's only a divorce. Death? Forget it."

Divorced. She'd wondered. "Why did you get divorced?"

"I loved my job more than my wife."

"That's an honest answer if I ever heard one."

"Life with an FBI negotiator is hard. At any time I could be called away for who knew how long. We were told to always have a bag packed and in our car. The final straw came at her brother's wedding. I got called in and had to leave. I came home from Manila two weeks later after negotiating the release of an oil company executive to find my wife had moved out."

"Harsh!" Janet's voice went half an octave higher than she'd aimed for and she smacked her lips together. "Sorry, but cripes, she didn't even tell you."

His lips bowed into a sagging smile. "She'd been telling me for months. I didn't listen. Or didn't care. I'm still not sure which. Either way, we're both better off. She remarried a nine-to-five guy and has a couple of kids now. She's happy. She deserves that."

He tried the phone again. No answer. "Damn. They won't pick up."

But Janet was still stuck on him being okay that his wife hadn't bothered to tell him she'd moved out while he'd been working. How could that be? When two people shared a life, how did communication break down to the point where one simply walked away without telling the other? "What do you deserve, Gavin?"

He flopped his bottom lip out. "Not sure. I guess I need someone who understands my life. I've chosen this work. I can't always control where I'll be and when. If I ever get married again, I'll have to make sure the person understands that."

He punched the button on the phone again. Waited. No answer.

"Keep trying." Janet wasn't sure if she meant the phone or about finding someone who understood his life. Which, she might add, she most certainly did.

"I never give up."

AFTER TWENTY MINUTES, SOMEONE PICKED UP. FINALLY. Gavin launched from his chair and snapped his fingers. Janet slid her headset on. Her task would be to analyze and research every morsel of information the hostage taker— HT—gave them.

"Joe?" Gavin said.

"Yeah."

"This is Gavin Sheppard."

"What are you people doing?"

"Well, Joe, we're trying to resolve this situation in a peaceful manner. We want everyone out of there safely."

"How the hell did you find us?"

"Joe, that doesn't matter. Let's stay focused here, okay? Try and fix this thing?"

"Will my article run in the paper?"

Gavin stared straight ahead. Above all, he always treated

the HT with respect. Earning their trust would help end the standoff and that meant being honest and decent. He wouldn't lie. Not yet, anyway. In a hostage situation, the first lie would come when he needed the HT to step in front of a window so the tactical team could get a clean shot.

"Joe, we've received your article and sent it to the newspaper."

Perfect non-answer.

"What did you do to our cell phones? We need our phones."

"We're trying to keep this situation under control. Look, Joe, you asked us not to call the authorities. We haven't done that. If we handle this ourselves, we'll all get what we want. How does that sound?"

Step up here, pal. Between the casual, anger-free speech and constantly using his first name, he was completely priming this guy.

"We want Jackson Spelling out of jail. He's been wrongly convicted. He's a great man and he's being persecuted by our government."

Yeah, dumbass, because he tried to kill a judge. Gavin rolled his eyes and sat. Sometimes this job made him sick, but he had to connect with this guy. Make him think he understood his rage. "Right, Joe. I hear ya. I was with the Bureau for twelve years. Why do you think I moved to the private sector? All that bureaucratic bullshit, that's why. The government, they want us all to be a bunch of puppets. Who needs that crap? Am I right?" He leaned back in the chair, jotted a note to himself.

Joe stayed silent. *Come on, idiot. Answer me so I can bury you.*

No answer.

"Tell your men outside to back off. We're leaving here."

Not gonna happen. If these people went mobile, they'd lose total control. And one thing Gavin never allowed was losing ground they'd already gained.

"Joe, right now, we need to talk about getting everyone out of this mess. I've directed our men surrounding the property to stay put. As long as you do the same and continue talking to me, nobody gets hurt. Nobody is hurt, right?"

"No. Nobody is hurt."

"Good, then we can end this thing right now. I get it, Joe. I know you want your guy freed, but I want you to do yourself a favor and walk out that front door."

"No."

A voice sounded in the background from the HT's end, but Gavin couldn't make it out. Then a muffling noise. Gavin motioned to Janet that Joe had placed his hand over the receiver. He made a note about the second person on the other end. Determining how many people were in that house would be his next task. Maybe he'd just lay it out there. He needed to keep this guy talking. Eventually, the boredom would wear him down and he'd give in.

"Joe, how many people do you have in there with you?"

The line went dead.

Damn.

Gavin went back to his notes. "We know there's at least one other person. We also know he's crapping his pants that we found them."

"For good reason," Janet said. "What now?"

"I need to keep him talking. If he's talking, he's not hurting Roxann. Best we can tell, he's in charge so we're dealing with the right person. What do we know about his family? Does he have a wife?"

"His tax returns say he's single but has one dependent."

"You got his tax returns?"

She grinned. "I have a friend at the IRS."

"I love you people. Maybe he's divorced. Or has a child from a previous relationship."

"He's twenty-nine, so either one is viable. I'm working on information on the dependent. Also, Joe works at an accounting firm."

"We have a current address for him, right?"

"Best that we can tell."

"Let's get someone to visit his office and his house to talk to his coworkers and neighbors. I need leverage with him. Maybe he's in a custody battle and wants to see his kid. I can use that."

Gavin tried the phone again.

Come on, Joe, pick up. Which someone did, but yelling from the other end echoed through the phone line—whoa—and Gavin straightened up. "Joe? It's Gavin. Everything all right?"

The line went dead.

Gavin tried again, but no answer. "Dammit. What the hell happened?"

"There's nothing on the monitor. Whatever it is, it's happening inside. Should we have the team take a look?"

He tried the phone again. "No. I need to get them calm again and they'll go nuts if they see a tactical team approach."

Someone picked up the other end. No yelling, but people were yapping at each other. "Joe? Talk to me. What do you need over there?"

"Nothing," Joe said. "Our *prisoner* just tried to run out the back door."

From the corner of his eye, he saw Janet look at him, her mouth partway open. *Don't look at her. Focus.*

"Well, Joe, you know, she's probably terrified. Let's get everyone to resume cool heads here, okay? Nobody is hurt, right?"

Agree with me, asshole. Agree with me.

"Nobody is hurt, but she won't be trying that again. Stupid bitch."

Something in the way he said *bitch* struck Gavin as wrong. Like maybe Joe Smith wasn't used to using colorful language. He made a note and stared at his notepad until the lines blurred. "What do you mean she won't try that again?"

"We were forced to *restrain* her. We were trying to go easy, but now she's chained to the bed. No more talking."

He hung up.

Gavin ripped his headset off, dumped it on the table and lowered himself to the folding chair. Next to him, Janet slowly peeled her headset away from her ear. "Well, just hell."

"Give her credit for trying, but we now have agitated hostage takers who chained a pregnant woman to a bed." He put his head down, ran two fingers over his forehead. "If one of them tries something, she may not even be able to defend herself. *Goddammit.*"

Janet reached over, touched his arm. "Take a break. A couple of minutes to regroup. That's all."

"If I regroup, they regroup."

She stuck her hand out, where his ancient iPod sat nestled in her palm. "Do it. Just a couple of minutes."

Most negotiators had a thing they did to decompress. Some exercised, some did puzzles, he listened to classical music. And she'd figured that out about him. He reached for the miniscule device, closed his hand over hers and squeezed. Their eyes met for a few brief seconds and he smiled.

She set her other hand over his and rubbed it slowly across the top. The motion settled his tortured mind. Or maybe it made it worse because now he was conjuring other uses for those lovely little hands.

What are you doing, Sheppard? Roxann Taylor is tied to a bed and this one is support staff. Problems everywhere and he was thinking about sex.

But—*yeah, it's getting hot in here*—that heat drilling right through him, teasing him, begging him to make a move.

"This is tough stuff," she said. "You're used to dealing with people you don't know. You're putting a lot of pressure on yourself. It's not fair that you need to do this, but I love watching you work. It's a noble thing and not many people could do it."

Make a move.

Janet beat him to it. Sure did. When she leaned forward and pressed her lips against his, he didn't necessarily fight it. He, in fact, threw himself into the fray. Specifically, his *tongue* threw them into the fray. Not that it could be considered bad. Women like her, who understood his crazy life and the stress he faced during a negotiation, yet still managed to make him smile, hadn't been in abundant supply for him.

She stirred something inside him and—weak-willed pig that he was—he wanted more. And then maybe more after that. *The spirit is willing, but the flesh is weak.*

Like every other good thing in his life, she backed away first, but settled her hand on his cheek. *Nice.*

"Wow," she said.

He smiled and pulled his hand away, the iPod clutched between his fingers. "I'll just take a minute to get my head together." *The one I need to get my boss's pregnant wife out of this.* "Let's not share this chained-to-the-bed thing, okay? We'll keep it between us? I don't want to ignite the situation."

She nodded. "Of course."

Sunlight shafted through the barn door and Vic stepped in. He took one look at Janet and halted. "What happened?"

3

———————

"Nothing happened," Janet said.

Vic assumed his arms-folded-scary-man stance. "You have that look you get when the shit is hitting the fan."

She had a look? News to her. She met his stare dead-on because her boss understood body language and if she turned away, he'd know she was hiding something. "I consider Roxann being kidnapped one giant episode of the shit hitting the fan. *That's* what happened."

Vic's gaze shifted to Gavin, then back to Janet. "You're sure?"

Suspicious.

But she wasn't sure of anything except that loaded-for-bear kiss she'd just planted on Sexy Galore. What an idiot she was. *Way to flush your career down the toilet, Janet.*

"Vic," she said, "I'm sure. What's the problem?"

He nodded, apparently not willing to fight. "Mike needs something to do. If he sits at the truck stop any longer, he's gonna go ape-shit. How are negotiations going?"

They're not.

Gavin stood and leaned back on the folding table. "Janet

just discovered some info on our HT. His tax records show he files single with a dependent. Let's get someone over to his house, see if we can get info to use as leverage."

Vic nodded. "Mike can do that."

Gavin gawked. "Tell me you're kidding."

"No. It'll keep him busy and out of your hair *and* he'll feel like he's contributing. He can handle it. Trust me."

Gavin looked at Janet. "What do you think? Can he do this without blowing his stack?"

The answer came to her in an instant. If anyone could, Michael was the person. He'd seen plenty of tragedy in his life. The man knew how to carry a load.

"He'll be fine."

Gavin held his hand to Janet who scribbled Joe Smith's address on a slip of paper and pressed it into his palm.

He read the address and gave it to Vic. "I hope you're right about this."

"We're right," Janet said. "No doubt."

Minutes later, after powering down his iPod, Gavin leaned against the barn door, staring off into the miles of cornfields surrounding the farm. The soft sway of the old oak tree soothed his mind and he breathed in the fresh, warm air. Country living. He might like it.

He watched Vic step out of his Tahoe after calling Mike with his assignment.

"We're good," Vic said. "He'll check out the address and call us."

A boom—*gunshot*—coming from the direction of the hostage location destroyed Gavin's moment of peace and he stood upright. His head hammered, the sound smacking against the inside of his skull and violating coherent thought. He hauled ass into the barn with Vic on his heels. "What was that?"

Janet shook her head. "Nothing on the radio."

Gavin grabbed his handheld from the table. "Alpha team. Report!"

"Who's firing?" Vic yelled.

"I don't know," Gavin said. "Didn't you tell them to stand down?"

"Back off. They know what they're doing. And yes, I told them."

He grabbed the second handheld from the table. "Status. Over."

"It came from the house, over."

What was this about? First Roxann trying to escape and now this? Jesus, the situation was collapsing. "Why is he firing?"

"My fault," someone said. "I wanted a better angle to the window and moved. They must have spotted me."

Gavin's blood pressure hit *launch* and he thought his head might disintegrate from the pulverizing pressure.

Dammit.

Fucking tactical guys always wanting to engage. Always wanting to go to guns. Always wanting a better shot.

"Stand down! Nobody fires until I get him on the phone."

Vic stood, arms crossed, waiting, and probably hoping this would be the event that would allow him to storm the place. *Keep waiting, pal.*

"Who the hell was it that moved?"

"Jessup," Vic said.

"Jessup!" Of all the fucking people he didn't expect to screw up, it was Peter "Monk" Jessup, by far the most reasonable of Vic's knuckle-draggers. That could only be classified as shocking. *Jesus.*

Vic grabbed a headset so he could listen in on Gavin's call to Joe. "One more shot from that house and we're going in."

The fuck we are. Gavin grabbed his headset. "Relax. Jessup shouldn't have been in motion." And then something inside him blew and the pressure behind his eyes butchered him. "I'm trying to build trust with this guy and your team has already shot that to hell."

"Hey!"

"Shut up!" Gavin roared just before Joe picked up the call. "Joe? What the hell happened? Who's firing?"

"Tell your men to back off!"

The squealing panic in Joe's voice? Not a good sign. Gavin breathed in, lowered himself to his chair. He had to repair the fractured trust. "Joe, let's calm down, okay? Nobody is going anywhere. Our guy wasn't trying to move on you. He was shifting around. Okay? You see that? Nobody is moving."

"I don't know."

"Take a minute and go look."

"So someone can shoot me? No way. You fucking federal guys are all the same."

"Joe, nobody is moving. My guy screwed up. He knows that."

"Yeah, he screwed up all right. Maybe I'll shoot this lady right now. How would that work? Then you people will take us seriously."

Gavin ignored Vic standing beside him, shaking his head. Just what he needed. A tense, emotional tactical guy. At the very least, he had to minimize the damage.

"Joe, you don't wanna do that. Right now, we can get you

out of this. I mean, yes, maybe you grabbed Mrs. Taylor, but you haven't hurt her, right? So, as long as nobody is hurt, we can resolve the situation. The police aren't involved. You could walk away from this. If someone gets hurt, then we have problems. Some jackass innocent bystander might be driving down the road and hear a gunshot. Before you know it, the cops are banging on your door. Am I right, Joe?"

Please say I'm right. No answer. Gavin took a moment to sort the chaos in his head into usable pieces. "Joe, listen to me, what you've done so far, it's not that bad. We can work out of it."

"What about getting Mr. Spelling released? I want someone to call me and tell me what time he'll be released."

Gavin took a breath. Back in business. "We're working on that. You didn't want the authorities involved so we need to go through back doors. It's gonna take a little while to get a hold of the people we need. That's all. How is everything else? Anything you need?"

"No."

"You sure, Joe? You've been holed up there a few hours. How about food? You got food in there?"

Silence. *They're hungry.* The one thing about hostage takers, they always needed something. Not necessarily wanted, but *needed.* Whether it was food or smokes or water. They always needed *something.*

"We could use hot food."

"No problem. Anything in particular? Pizza? Sandwiches?"

"Pizza. Three of them. Extra large."

Three? Gavin made a note and did a quick calculation in his head. On a good night he could put away a medium pizza on his own. But he'd have to be famished. Three extra-large pizzas meant at least, *at least,* three people. And that number probably didn't include Roxann.

"Sure," Gavin said. "How about drinks? We'll bring you some pops. What do you guys like?"

"We need a Mountain Dew, some bottled waters, a Coke and iced tea. And whatever the lady likes. I don't care."

Three different drinks, plus the waters. "Give us thirty minutes and I'll call you back to arrange delivery."

"You're not coming near this house!"

"We're gonna talk about that. We'll leave the food somewhere and you can grab it. How would that be?"

The line went dead and Gavin removed his headset.

"Head-shrinker, what are you doing?"

Gavin held up his hand while he read over his notes. "Based on this food order, I'm guessing we've got at least three people, probably four, plus Roxann inside. I need to find out how many guns they have." He handed over the food order. "Get this food while I work out a delivery plan."

Vic snatched the slip of paper from him. "One of my guys delivers the food."

"No. They'll see a tactical guy and go balls to the wall. That's the last thing we need."

"Actually," Vic argued, "that's exactly what we need. These fuckers think they're in charge. Let's show them what kind of manpower they're up against."

"Guys," Janet said, "arguing won't get Roxann free."

But Gavin had his sights on Vic. "We've just learned new information and you need to stand down while I work through it."

"Oh? What have we learned?"

Gavin stood taller, took a small step toward Vic. "They've just proven to us they're not afraid to use their guns."

· · ·

CRAVING FRESH AIR AND SENSING HER BOSS'S NEED TO VENT, Janet walked outside with Vic for a chat before he made the food run. She walked to his Tahoe with him and leaned against it, the heat from the front quarter panel seeping through her slacks. Hot day. "Gavin knows what he's doing."

Vic huffed out a breath. "Great, you too? Bad enough Mike is on his side."

"No sides here, remember? All I know is Roxann is in that house. And she's pregnant and I'm terrified for her. I think it would be a good idea if you gave Gavin a wee bit of room to do his job. He's a reasonable man. Plus, the deal was, he'd have until nightfall to talk these guys down. That's another four hours from now."

"And what if something happens before then? How do any of us live with it if she doesn't walk out of there when we could have taken these assholes down?"

"How do you know she won't get hurt in the takedown?"

He stared at her a second too long. "Vic, I know you think you can haul in there and save her. I've been around you guys long enough to get that, but I've seen what Gavin can do. Give him a break and quit bugging him so he can concentrate."

"You do remember I'm your boss."

"Yes, but there are times you need to be slapped." She grinned. "I'm happy to do the slapping."

He rolled his eyes. "Two things. First, get off my damned truck. Second, I'll stay quiet until nightfall. Only because you asked me."

"Gee, my hero. Bring back extra food for us."

"Yes, ma'am."

He climbed into the Tahoe and fired the engine. With that task completed, Janet spun on her heel to have a go at Gavin and a food delivery plan. She was getting sick of these two squabbling and if she could help Gavin come up with a plan Vic might agree to, they'd all get some semblance of peace in an otherwise crappy day.

Entering the barn, she found Gavin slouched back in the folding chair with his feet propped on the table. The man had the ability to look completely relaxed, but she knew his mind was active. She leaned on the table to face him. "What are you thinking about the food delivery?"

"I'd like to leverage it to get a look at Roxann. Make sure she's okay. But they're not gonna let us anywhere near the house, which means Roxann would have to come out. I doubt they'll let that happen. I'll deliver the food."

"Vic will freak. He'll want to do it or have one of the guys do it."

"I know. They'll use it as an excuse to get closer to the house. I can't risk it. I have to rebuild trust and sending in someone in full-blown tactical gear won't do it."

"I'll do it."

"Uh, no."

"Why not? Gavin, look at me. I'm tiny. I look weak and harmless. Send me up the driveway with the food. I'll stand there and they open the door so I can see Roxann. Once I see she's okay, I'll leave."

He puckered then shook his head. "Too dangerous."

"I disagree. I think, of all our options, this one is the least dangerous. Plus, Vic won't argue over it."

"Yeah, he will."

Had a point there. "You're right. He will, but I can convince him. I've worked for him for four years. And whether he'll admit it or not, he's afraid of me."

Gavin gawked. "Really?"

"Of course. Whatever secrets I don't know about this

bunch—" she waggled her fingers, "—I can find with a computer."

"God, I love how you people work."

You haven't seen anything yet. "I'm small, but I'm mighty."

He twisted his lips, clearly trying to hide a grin. Making Gavin Sheppard smile had to be one of the few highlights in this miserable day.

"You are indeed."

For thirty-six minutes they debated the merits of her plan until Gavin finally gave in. He may not have been completely on board, but he knew the only option Vic could be convinced of was her playing pizza delivery girl.

"You'll support me on this?" Janet asked.

He stared at her from his seat, his gaze connecting with hers. "As much as I hate it, yes."

A car crunching over gravel outside alerted them to Vic's return. She stepped to the barn door and spotted him carrying four pizza boxes and a bag—probably the drinks.

"Hi," Janet said.

He stepped into the barn and dumped the boxes on the table. "What's the plan?"

Gavin waited a second for Vic to step over to where he sat. Nice power play there, making the big man come to him. Janet almost laughed out loud over the posturing these two did.

"First," Gavin said, "let me finish before you comment. I have no doubt you'll have issues with this idea, but you need to think it through."

"Fine."

Gavin nodded. "I would like to leverage the food delivery to get a look at Roxann. They insist she's fine, but I want proof."

"Agreed," Vic said.

"I'm trying to build trust again. If they see one of the tactical team coming at them, they're going to blow their minds."

"Oh," Vic said. "I'm gonna fucking hate this."

"Hey," Janet interrupted. "You said you'd listen."

He held up his hands. *Good boy.*

"Janet will deliver the food."

"Fuck no," Vic said.

Janet raised her hand. "I know I'm not a tactical person, but look at me. First off, I'm a woman. That alone will reduce the tension. Second, they'll see how small I am and think I'm harmless."

"We'll put her in a vest and helmet, to be sure. I hate it as much as you do. Last thing I want is her in harm's way."

"I'll be fine. I'll look like a peanut in Kevlar. They won't see me as a threat."

Vic assumed his arms-folded-don't-mess-with-me stance that drove most people to urination. "I don't like it."

"You don't have to."

Janet held her hand out to shut Gavin up. "Vic, you have to see the possibilities. If you can do that, you'll realize this is the best way to ease tension *and* ensure Roxann is okay."

Vic stared at her, but kept quiet. *Come on, boss. Let me do this.*

"You're okay with this?"

She jerked her head. "Yes. I can help and if it keeps the situation level, I'm absolutely okay with it."

The man was still her immediate supervisor and she wanted him to sign off. For whatever reason, she yearned for his support.

"You'll wear a vest and a helmet and take a radio." He turned to Gavin. "I want a show of force. We're putting an army of guys at the end of the driveway, in full gear, making sure she stays safe. I want them to see us and know if they hurt her, they're going down. Do your head-shrinking and convince them it's for her protection and if they don't fire, we won't."

That, at least, sounded reasonable.

Gavin nodded. "I'll work it out. Get her into a vest and helmet."

He went to the phone and initiated contact.

Janet approached the house on trembling legs. She focused on the front door and, as much as she despised her own weakness, fear quickly gobbled every ounce of bravery. How did Vic's guys do this all the time? Some people might thrive on it, but this experience proved she wasn't one of them.

No. What she wanted was to set this food down, see Roxann and run like hell.

"You're doing great," Gavin said via the earpiece in her right ear.

She breathed in.

Sure Joe Smith promised she wouldn't get hurt as long as she came no closer than fifty feet, but who knew if he could be trusted? The man was a kidnapper. She concentrated on the weight of the Kevlar protecting her and pushed her shoulders back.

Even if they shot at her, chances were she'd survive. Doing this had been her idea and now she wondered if she'd live through it.

With each step she ignored the growing urge to glance behind her where Monk, Billy, Bobby and four other armed team members dressed in riot gear stood behind the cover of an SUV. Gavin and Vic sat in the car on the edge of the property, but she didn't look at them. Didn't need to. She knew they were there. Her immediate task was to estimate fifty feet from the house and leave the food. Then she'd raise her arms, the hostage takers would open the front door and allow her to see Roxann.

Done deal.

She kicked a stone, watched it fly and said a silent thanks for the distraction. Three more steps. Fifty feet or not, the covered front porch was just ahead and her hammering pulse told her to stop. She'd leave the food and back up until the kidnappers opened the door.

This is it.

Slowly, she set the food and drinks on the ground. With even more care, she straightened and raised her arms.

"Food is set," someone said through the radio.

Don't think about the fear. She counted the seconds until the front door opened.

Two, three, four, five...

Inch by inch, the faded blue front door opened, but...

No one.

Come on.

And then Roxann stepped into the doorway. If she'd gotten closer, Janet imagined she'd see lines of fatigue on Roxann's face, but from this distance—God bless her—she still managed to look amazing. Her long blond hair was pulled back and she wore black shorts and a summer-weight white sweater. *Right.* She'd been on her way to the lake house.

"Hi," Janet called. "Are you okay?"

Roxann turned her head to the left and her mouth moved. Probably asking permission to answer. She turned back to Janet. "I'm okay. Tell Michael I love him and I'm sorry."

"Nothing to be sorry about. We're working on getting you out."

Someone reached from behind the wall, grasped Roxann's arm and yanked her from the door before slamming it.

Just that fast, a woman she'd grown to admire, to respect for her demanding career and her ability to lead a staff composed of mostly men, a woman Janet dreamed of growing into, had been snatched from sight. Completely unfair.

All Roxann had done was marry a powerful man. That, combined with working her ass off to succeed in her own high-profile position, made her a target. Add in her pregnancy and the harsh reality of this horrid event and—man-oh-man—it fired a spitting, seething anger that charred Janet from deep inside.

Was this what dedication to the job resulted in? Janet had spent immeasurable time worrying, thinking, worrying more about her career and what people thought of her. How they *viewed* her. In the end, would it really matter? At this moment, did it matter to Roxann?

Who knew?

Afraid to turn her back to the door, Janet walked backward. What a sight she must be.

Tac vest.

Helmet.

Walking backward.

"You're almost there," Gavin said via the radio. "Doing great. Just don't trip," he cracked.

If she wasn't shivering from fear and that fierce, scorching anger she'd blast him.

"We're ten steps behind you," Monk said.

God, she loved that guy. Leave it to him to find a way to let her feel protected while being totally exposed.

And then she was there, stepping behind the SUV between Monk and Billy.

Mission accomplished. Roxann was, for the most part, okay.

And no one was dead.

Gavin jumped out of Vic's SUV and opened the back door for Janet. Cool air wrapped around her and she swiped at the sweat on her neck. Whether that sweat came from fear, anger or heat—maybe all—she couldn't be certain. Gavin stood, the open car door at his back, watching her as she swung her helmet off, tossed it on the seat and went to work on the vest. Despite her appreciation of its function, she absolutely hated it. The idea of wearing something that stopped bullets freaked her out. Seeing Roxann a prisoner freaked her out. The whole damned situation freaked her out.

"I've got Mike on speaker," Vic said and, not wanting to waste time, Gavin jumped into the backseat with Janet.

His knee bumped hers and he grabbed her leg. "Sorry."

Janet stared straight ahead. *Didn't feel a thing.* That little buzz was adrenaline. That was all.

"Did you see Rox?" Michael asked.

Good. Concentrate on Michael and his pregnant wife. "She looks good. Tired, obviously, but you know your wife, she's a powerhouse. I think I want to be her when I grow up."

Silence drifted through the phone line. "Did you talk to her?"

"I did. She said she was fine and to tell you that she loved you and she was sorry."

Again, he stayed silent. Janet didn't like that. This man was their leader, their safe-haven when the atrocities they faced overwhelmed her, and she didn't want him in pain. Not for one second.

Fill that quiet.

"Michael, for what she's going though, she looked amazing. I think, as crazy as this will sound, they must be treating her okay."

Aside from the fact they have her chained to a bed. He didn't need that four-one-one, though.

"What's next?" Michael wanted to know.

"Head-shrinker, I'll take you and Janet back to the barn. I'm gonna rotate teams here and take alpha team out to our farm. I'll leave Monk, Billy and Bobby V. with you. Monk will take command while I'm gone."

Vic taking the team to Taylor Security's training center would not be good news for Gavin. Having worked around these guys, Janet understood how hard they trained and practiced and practiced more for takedowns.

"We're not there yet," Gavin said.

Vic drove to the barn, but didn't bother parking. "Understood, but I want them sharp if something comes up. Mike, what have you got on the HT?"

"He has a nine-year-old son with a former girlfriend. They were college sweethearts, but broke up when the kid was ten months. His coworkers say he's a loner. Eats lunch at his desk. Rarely joins them unless it's a company function. Sometimes not even then."

Gavin jotted notes on his pocket notepad as Michael spoke. As a certified geek herself, Janet made an educated guess that Joe Smith, with his love of reading and playing on the computer, had probably been a bullied kid who found solace on his own.

"Got it," Gavin said. "Anything about who's raising the boy?"

"Shared custody. It seems loose. The neighbor said the boy is around a lot. Then she clammed up. She didn't believe I was his distant cousin."

"Nice," Vic said.

Gavin finished his notes. "Thanks. I can work with this."

"Vic," Michael said, "I'll meet you at the farm."

Once again, Janet marveled at the strength it must have taken for Michael, with his abundant protective instincts, to stay away from the place of his wife's imprisonment. Realistically, the husband of a hostage, no matter how controlled, brought emotional chaos to an already toxic situation. Michael understood that.

Gavin pushed the car door open. "We'll keep you updated. Vic, tell the guys they did good. Not that they need to hear it from me, but they should know."

Janet jumped from the Tahoe—where exactly was her stepladder? So damned short. She felt like a five-year-old.

Dammit.

Gavin grabbed the tac vest from her. "It weighs more than you do."

She laughed at that. At least something made her laugh.

He pulled the barn door open and she stopped, stared inside a minute. Call her selfish, but she didn't want to go back in there. As if not going in would make the situation disappear.

Gavin leaned on the door and crossed his arms. "It's understandable. To be unnerved."

Oh, oh, oh, unbelievable how well he could read people.

"I'm fine."

He nodded.

"What?"

Now a shrug. "Nothing. You seem upset. I wanted you to know it's okay to give in to the stress. Some of the toughest guys I know would be terrified to do what you did."

Total God. That's what he was. So much for her quest not to turn stupid. Ignoring him, she walked into the barn. He followed and closed the door behind them. Odd. With this heat, any additional air in the musty old barn would be a blessing. He dropped the vest on the large folding table and she held her hands out. "What now?"

"We wait. Let them get their bellies full and then I go at them again. Food tends to relax people. You did great, by the way."

She smiled at him and yes, maybe she was staring. She couldn't help it. After all that fear and the crazy adrenaline it unleashed, something inside her blew open.

Sexy.

Galore.

Wow. This raging need must be what the guys felt after seeing action. Talk about a meltdown. And the thing she wanted—right now—was to be free of the accumulated searing heat and sadness and anger. She stepped forward.

"It did freak me out. Seeing Roxann like that. As women go, she's my hero. She's everything I've never been. Tall, beautiful, savvy, successful. She's an Olympic gold medalist and now she's a pregnant hostage. For all of her strength, she's as vulnerable as a woman can be. It's not fair."

His gaze still on her, Gavin stepped closer. "You're right."

"And I've spent all this time worrying about my career and what people think of me. Trying to prove I'm not the geeky, awkward girl hiding behind a computer because I don't understand people. I mean, what am I doing? I'm not a teenager. When I looked at Roxann, I realized none of it should matter. For all her success, she might not walk away from this. I don't want to waste my life worrying about dumb..." she flapped her hands. "Dumb...*shit* when it could all end at any time. I've spent years trying to be the unslut."

He shook his head like he didn't understand. *Join the club, big guy.*

"The *un*slut?"

"It's the reverse of a slut. I don't sleep with the operators. Some women in this company do. I mean, yeah, from a woman's point of view, I can see why, but I've worked too hard to destroy my career by not keeping my legs closed." She met his gaze. "Until now."

Yeesh. So confused. *What am I doing?* Nothing like making oneself look truly pathetic. She waved it off. "Ignore me. Emotional vomit."

Smart girl gone stupid. Somehow it always involved Gavin.

"Slow down and give yourself a break. All those things you said about Roxann? Some women would say that about you. You work with guys two and three times your size and you're not intimidated. Every guy on Vic's team knows not to screw with you. They understand your value and that your skills will—and have—saved their lives. Those women in the business office? They're jealous. You earned your job with your skills instead of on your back. They don't under-stand that."

He knew about the witch twins. She opened her mouth. Nothing. Nada. Not one coherent sentence.

He huffed. "Yeah. I know about them. They're vile women who thrive on gossip and you don't need them. They know it and that's why they hate you. It has nothing to do with you being a geek, and everything to do with you not kissing their asses."

Total head-shrinker. She didn't care. *Stupid, stupid girl.*

She stepped toward him, got close enough to feel the heat of his body. "I'm all screwed up."

He leaned back. Only a little. "I respectfully agree with you."

Inching forward, she tugged on his shirt. "But I'm done thinking."

He held up his hands. "What are we talking about here?"

Finally, an easy question. "Sex. If you ask me, *we've* been thinking too much. Maybe we just need to get it over with. Get it out of our systems."

He laughed. "You think *that's* what we need?"

She flipped the button on her pants. "Yep."

The button got his attention and he stared at it a second before looking back at her. "What if we don't get it out of our systems? What then?"

"Then we keep going until we do."

"That seems logical to you?"

"Not one bit. But it's what I want. It's what you want. I feel it and until we expend it, we'll be driven crazy. And if I have to sit here thinking about it while our hostage takers eat, well, that's way too much thinking time. Way. Too. Much. As I just said, I don't want to waste any more time thinking."

She didn't see any point in denying it, but Gavin? His olive skin had gone white and she'd been around him enough to know his brain had one heck of a violent hockey game going.

Minimize.

Something he'd taught her about negotiating. "Gavin, this is not life or death. I'm talking about easing tension. We're in this crappy situation, I just nearly peed myself in fear and I need to be held. You're the one I want to hold me."

Seemed pretty straightforward to her so she reached for

her zipper and bit by bit, with Gavin's eyes on her hand making that slow descent, she unzipped her pants.

GAVIN NEARLY BAWLED. WHAT THE HELL WAS HE DOING? Actually, he wasn't the one doing it. *He* stood letting *her* do it. Totally sandbagged. As much as the upstanding guy inside him wanted to convince her, and himself, they were coworkers and shouldn't do this, he couldn't get the words out. Not even a syllable.

Struck mute by an erection, that's what he was.

After a pain-in-the-ass day of arguing with the knuckle-dragger and dealing with the emotional barrage of Roxann being snatched, maybe he did need a tension buster.

Why not? For the past three weeks he'd thought about nothing but making love to her.

He hadn't counted on it being in a dusty old barn, but maybe this was the way it should be. They'd been confined all day, trying to reunite a loving couple and dealing with the emotional crap that came with it. Now they were alone with nothing to do but kill time.

Let's kill time.

Decision made. He eased his arms around her and held his breath. At that first bit of contact he hesitated, tried to calm his rioting brain and take it all in because, yes, they were going to do this and he was going to let it happen.

Maybe it would be more than a quick lay. Maybe he'd get lucky and this crazy hunger he'd been trying to bury for three weeks would change his life in a way he'd never antici-pated. A good way, a promising way he wanted to explore. Yep, he needed to capture and catalogue the crazy gut-squeeze that came with his hand molding so perfectly over her hip, and the way her tiny body curved into his larger one, the way he flashed hot then cold when she touched him. With her, all the extremes descended on him at once.

He bent low to kiss her. Jeez, she was a little bit of a woman, but that didn't stop her from angling her mouth over his, her tongue darting in and out in a blazing assault. The little bit of a woman had a monster-sized libido.

Jackpot, brother.

Within seconds, she stepped back, tore her shirt over her head and tossed it. The bra went next and he found himself staring at the perfect proportions of her small, amazingly torturous breasts.

Whatever you do, don't break her. That's what he worried about? Breaking her? *How about risking your job, Mr. Sexual Harasser?*

Her pants went next and she hopped around on one foot kicking out of them, making him grin while he tore his shirt over his head. Horndog that he was, the sexual harasser wasn't just going for it, he was damned near willing to beg.

She paddled her hands. "We should make it fast, right?"

"Afraid the knuckle-dragger will walk in on us?"

"Oh, my God! That would be hilarious in the most disgusting way imaginable. His eyes would bleed."

"Maybe we'll take our time."

The snorting sound she made should not have been attractive, in any way, but—hell's sake—everything about her made him smile. This tiny woman with the giant heart and funny quirks made him want nothing more than to be with her night and day. He could spend every available minute enjoying her. That's how easy being around her could be.

"Gavin, quit staring and strip. Tick-tock. I really don't want my boss seeing me naked." She threw her hands out, her face scrunched. "Ew! That would be bad. I'd be my own reality show. Smart girl gone ultra-stupid."

And now he flat-out laughed. "Are you always this talkative when you're about to get laid?"

"If my boss is about to walk in? I'd imagine so. Get those pants off."

Gavin did as he was told and kicked out of his pants.

"Yay," she said, making him laugh again when she wiggled her fingers at him. "Come to Mama, sweetheart."

"Seriously, you have to stop with that. It's creeping me out how turned on I am by it."

And then she jumped him. Literally. Jumped into his arms, wrapping her legs around his waist and kissing him in a full-out assault that had nothing to do with patience and everything to do with lust.

Any chance he had of backing out dissolved into a puddle of his own need—hell, he was a guy—and he carried her to the cot while shoving her underwear over her butt. Damn he liked how she felt against him. All that warm, soft skin. He tossed the crappy cot mattress to the floor and set her down while she wiggled out of her underwear and he dug a condom from his wallet.

"Yay!" she said again, hooking her hand around his neck and dragging him on top of her. "We can go slow next time."

Next time. "*Yay!*" he mimicked.

4

———

When Gavin pushed into her, a giant, engulfing tornado looped around her, sucking her into its vortex. After all the lectures she'd inflicted upon herself. Here they were, going at it like farm animals.

In a barn.

How appropriate.

She wouldn't fool herself into thinking they were making love. Maybe this crazy heat between them would only be sex in the purest, hottest, neediest form, but that was okay.

Sometimes, like right now, it was just fine.

At least she thought so. And then he slowly slid out of her and she opened her eyes, smiling up at him smiling down at her. "Are you teasing me?"

"I hope so."

She clamped her hands on his butt. "I'm small but I'm mighty."

Then he kissed her, all soft and warm and slow and her brain melted. A quick flash of what used to be a smart girl who had done the one thing she swore she would not do.

But, oh, oh, oh, she hadn't counted on wanting Gavin Sheppard and dreaming of him the way she had since that amazing first kiss.

And she began to tremble from the force of all that emotion bombarding her, making her want more and more and more.

She wanted this always. With him.

Stop thinking.

Yes. She had to. All this coming undone, thinking about the ways her career could end and yet, at the moment, it would all be worth it. It felt that good. Never before had it felt that good.

He touched her face, just a light slide of three fingers over her cheek and something cracked—an insane snapping inside her head—and she pulled him tighter into her.

So good.

The pace quickened and that crazy snapping whipped through her body. *More.*

In a rush of grunts and murmurs they dove over the edge together, Janet clinging to him, almost afraid to open her eyes. It might, in fact, all be a dream. Or, depending on how she looked at it, a nightmare, because after this, she would no doubt be chasing him around the office.

With her pants down.

She cracked up. *So stupid, Janet.* Funny, but stupid.

But then his breath hitched and he kissed the side of her head and she did open her eyes.

Fantastic.

Delight swarmed her and she grinned up at the ceiling. "I would like more please." *So much more.*

Gavin let out a heavy breath. "Insatiable, are you?"

"Never before. Apparently with you I am. Is that a problem?"

"Not in this lifetime."

But then he eased off her, dropping a kiss on the tip of her nose, then her lips. "I adore you. Even if you accuse me of sexual harassment."

She shoved him off with a laugh. "I think I was the harasser. Totally guilty."

"But I loved it."

Their gazes met for a split-second, two people riding the high of a couple of healthy orgasms. Janet rolled sideways to retrieve her scattered clothing. If she did it fast enough, maybe they could forego the whole wow-we-shouldn't-have-done-that routine.

"You okay?" he asked.

She slipped her bra on, trying not to stare while Gavin retrieved his pants. "You have no idea how great I am. I shouldn't feel this good. Not with Roxann in trouble, but I'm not going to overthink it. Let's just get her out of there."

Janet took her seat, slid her headset on and forced herself not to think about the potentially colossal mistake she'd just made. Not that the sex wasn't swoon worthy, but hello? She'd broken her most important career girl rule and boffed an executive. Worse, she wanted to do it again.

Many times.

"Yeah, well," she muttered. *Too late to worry about it.* Besides, it was fun.

Gavin picked up his headset to call Joe Smith. "What?"

She looked at him. "What, what?"

"You said something."

"I did?"

He laughed. "Yes."

She nodded and went back to her laptop to see if she could find and hack into Joe Smith's bank account. Why not? "I'm dandy."

He set his hand on her shoulder. "Are you freaking out again?"

And, oh, this man.

Sexy.

Galore.

"It's sinking in. I mean, I don't do this and now I'm afraid you think I'm the reverse unslut." The reverse unslut? What the heck? *Lost my damned mind.* Total emotional vomit. Or maybe she was simply terrified of falling in love with him.

He shook his head and laughed. "I don't think you're the reverse unslut. Although, I'm not sure I understand what that is. What I think is you and I have chemistry that rumbles a house and we need to figure out what to do with it. You don't want to be the reverse unslut and I don't want to be the executive who hounds female employees."

"This was more my doing than yours."

He held up his hand. "It doesn't matter. We don't want people gossiping, so let's table the discussion until we get Roxann released. Okay?"

"You're right. I'm sorry."

"Nothing to be sorry about." He waved a hand between them. "I don't see us as a bad thing. I just don't know how to handle it. Yet."

Welcome to Awkwardville. She motioned to the throw phone. "We can figure it out later."

After I hang myself because I can't stop chasing you around the office with my pants down.

Gavin initiated the call to Joe. That fast he'd switched gears. Amazing. Janet adjusted her headset and settled in to listen and take notes.

"Joe?" Gavin said into the phone. "How was dinner? Everything quiet there?"

"Yeah," Joe said. "Where are we on Mr. Spelling's release?"

"We're working on that. The *Banner* has confirmed they received your article. They're looking at it."

Not a total lie on his part.

"By the way, Joe, is there anyone you need me to call? Anywhere you should be? Family maybe?"

Maybe she shouldn't be feeling smug, but Gavin was so playing this guy. *Going down, sucker.*

"Uh, no. I'm good."

"No family?"

"I...uh...have a son. He's with my mother now."

Going.

Down.

Sucker.

"A son. That's awesome. I don't have any kids. Always wanted them, but haven't found the right girl yet."

I could be that girl. But she didn't dare look at him. No, siree. She would keep focused on her notes. If she looked at him now, she'd not only be the smart girl turned stupid, she'd be nominated for president of the nonprofit organization Stupid Girls Unite.

"My son is nine," Joe said. "Plays Little League baseball. Kid loves baseball."

From the corner of her eye, she glanced at Gavin, kicked back in his chair, arms folded across his chest like this was just a casual chat. And yet, hadn't they just talked about him playing catch with his dad? The man's ability to compartmentalize ranked right up there with Michael's.

"Oh, hey," Gavin said. "I can relate. When I was a kid all I ever wanted was to throw a ball with my dad. Maybe shag some flies. Nothing better than that."

I could love him. She shook off that potentially life-bombing thought because really, she shouldn't be sitting here imagining him playing catch with their children. And who said they were having more than one?

Pay attention! She smacked herself—hard—on the head and Gavin looked over, his face twisted.

Sorry, she mouthed and he nodded.

I accept the presidency. Thank you.

"You know what though, Joe?"

"What?"

Gavin slowly leaned forward, a panther bearing down. "What do you think your son would want you to do now?"

"Huh?"

"I think he would want you to walk out of that house, right? My dad was gone by my fourteenth birthday and you know what? I never got over that. Do your son a favor and come out of there before someone gets hurt. No one is hurt. What you've done isn't all that bad. We can minimize this and your son will have his father."

And, God, Janet was dying inside, her heart aching for Gavin as a little boy craving his father and somehow, when she looked at grown-up Gavin, he seemed relaxed, kicked back, just shooting the bull with a buddy.

Then he turned to her, literally shifting his body in his chair to settle that dark gaze on her and she yearned to curl into him. To soothe the suffering little boy who'd lost his father.

He pushed the mute button on the phone. "Can you find me the son?"

Varying thoughts slammed inside her head. *Snap out of it.* What was she doing? This was the game he played. His *job.* He probably wasn't even thinking about his own father and she was what? Imagining they'd have some huge epiphany that she'd be the one to round out his lonely life?

Please.

She spun to her laptop. "Of course. I'll track down Joe's ex."

"You don't know anything about my son," Joe said.

No, but he will in three minutes.

Gavin pushed the button on the phone again. "You're right. But I was nine once, and I had a father I loved very much. I missed a lifetime of memories with my dad. Do you want that for your son?"

"No, but this is important. Jackson Spelling doesn't deserve to be in jail."

"Joe, let's concentrate on you, and what we can do to get you out of this mess. Get you home to that little boy of yours. Can we do that?"

"I don't know."

Janet kept at the code to crack into Joe's ex-girlfriend's Facebook page. So close. So darned close. "Almost there," she whispered. "Come to Mama."

"And how about your mom?" Gavin said to Joe. "Are you close with her? Must be if you let her watch your son."

"Yeah. I'm pretty close with her. She takes great care of my son."

"It's gotta be tough being a single dad. I give you credit. It's good you have support from your mom. Jeez, Joe, you've got a great family."

"It's a decent life."

Gavin sat forward and stared straight ahead. "Even more reason to think about what you're doing here. I get that you feel Jackson Spelling is being persecuted, I do. Maybe I can help you with that after we get you out of there safely."

"You can get us out of here by getting our leader out of jail."

A click sounded on the other end of the phone line.

.   .   .

GAVIN SNATCHED HIS HEADSET OFF AND SHOT OUT OF HIS chair to walk off some energy. He eyeballed the iPod on the desk, but decided against it. "Damn. Thought I had him."

"I thought you did too. It seemed like you were so close."

He held his hands out. "That's how it goes sometimes. You think you have them and—poof—gone." He checked his watch. Almost 7:00 p.m. *Shit.* "Anything on the son?"

"Give me one second. I'm about to grab the mother's cell number."

"Excellent."

This woman was amazing. Made his life so much easier. And she made him laugh. Not an easy thing to accomplish lately. He grinned at her, this cute pixie who was fearless in her job and did battle with men two and a half times her body weight. His chest expanded, a huge burst of something opening up inside him and filling him with respect and adoration for someone he had no business feeling that way about.

It is what it is. If he was anything, he was a realist. By all indications after the gymnastic sex not half an hour ago, neither one of them would be interested in running away from said situation. Yes, he was an executive and she was support staff. No, she didn't report to him. If they handled it carefully, it could work.

He'd make it work.

Janet handed him a slip of paper. "Here you go. The ex's number. What are you going to do?"

He stared down at the digits, contemplated the destruction they could cause. How Joe would react to seeing his son, Gavin couldn't guess. The pressure, the emotional warfare, might be too much. Maybe he'd commit suicide.

Maybe he'd drag the kid in as a hostage. Maybe he'd turn a gun on a pregnant Roxann Taylor.

Who knew what drove people in these situations?

Gavin ran a hand over his head. "It's a hip-shot." He stopped walking, looked at Janet and imagined how it would feel if she were the one chained to a bed. Rotting, foul sickness consumed him. Decision made. "I want the son here. This guy loves his son and the kid might slap some sense into him. Emotionally speaking."

"It's getting late. You may not have time."

"Has Vic made contact?"

"No, but they'll be back soon."

Janet slid the headset off and set it down on the desk. She leveled her hand over it and tapped her fingers. This wouldn't be good. "Go ahead. Say it."

She raised her gaze to him and their eyes held. That brief hesitation, the pinched tight lips, left no doubt she was struggling to find the right words.

The ones that wouldn't piss him off.

"I think you need to prepare yourself. Vic held up his end, and he'll come in here, literally, with guns blazing. The deal was nightfall and that time is approaching. I know him. Once it's nightfall, there will be no debates."

"I'm not done yet. I almost had Joe. I felt it. That's why he hung up."

"I realize that, but he—*they*—haven't agreed to surrender."

Surrender. Not a word negotiators used. Hostage takers interpreted surrendering as a negative thing. Jail. Courtrooms. Either way, it meant failure.

But Janet was right. He didn't have the kind of time he would need to drag this guy out of there with words alone.

Unless...

He spun to the barn door. Janet had opened it and the waning sunlight splashed across the entry. The quiet surrounded him and the smell of fresh air cleared his mind. *Go for it.* He whipped back to Janet. "I need to get face-to-face with him. And I need his son with me."

She jumped from her chair. *"What?"*

"If I can show him the kid, then get in a room with this guy, I can talk him out. He'll keep thinking about his son and he'll walk out. He's nuts about this kid and won't want him to see him this way."

"Gavin, you're crazy if you think I'm letting you go in there. You have no idea what kind of weaponry they have. You could walk through the front door and get shot. You may not even make it to the front door! They might shoot you in the driveway."

"Not if I have his son next to me. I think I connected with him on the kid. We'll get the team to line up like they did when you delivered the food. I'll tell Joe I'm coming in to talk and I'll have another go at him."

Both her hands went straight up. "Oh, no. No. No. No. Vic will go *crazy.*"

"He's not here. When he gets back, he can call me on the radio and scream, but this is a good idea. If I get in a room with these people, I can talk them out. I can also get a look at the interior and maybe see Roxann. If we wind up breaching, we'll need that intel."

Yes. This was a plan he could live with. Gavin picked up his cell phone to call the child's mother.

Janet paced the barn while Gavin talked with Joe's ex-girlfriend. *He can't do this.* The raging panic pounded her and she dragged her palms up her forehead. There he was, sitting in that damned crappy folding chair, his feet propped on the makeshift desk while she had a grand mal seizure.

He's insane.

She should step outside and call Vic. Shouldn't she? Let him know about this half-baked plan? Maybe Vic was close and could talk him out of it.

The sex *really* must have turned her stupid because after all the arguing she'd heard today, Gavin would never allow Vic, of all people, to talk him out of a turkey sandwich, much less meeting with a hostage taker. It would be a whole new ballistic missile thrown into an already tenuous working relationship.

But, dammit, she wanted Gavin out of harm's way. With this plan, he'd be locked in the jaws of it.

No.

Finally, Gavin hung up and she wasted no time. "You can't go in there. You have no idea what this guy will do when he sees his son. What about the people with him? We don't know anything about them." She stepped to him, grabbed both his hands and squeezed. "I know you hate the idea of going tactical, but this is too extreme. Let Vic win this one. Please."

To his credit, he remained seated rather than taking a position of strength by standing over her. "It's not about winning. It's about making sure a pregnant woman goes home to her husband. If we go tactical, I have no confidence, no matter how good I know our team is, that Roxann won't get hurt. I'm not worried about our side. It's the people in the house that concern me. They're unstable. I think if I put this guy's son in front of him, the love for his child will trump this crazy-assed mission they're on."

"You think?"

Gavin nodded. "Never any guarantees, but my instincts are good. Better than good. This is the way to go."

All this, she knew. When Gavin left the FBI, he'd been one of their top three negotiators. Six months ago, he'd joined Taylor Security and on his first day, after he'd been introduced to the team, she hacked into his employee file. Not something she was proud of but she'd convinced herself it was idle curiosity about the new guy. Now, months later, she didn't bother denying she'd been attracted to him the second she'd seen him. He'd walked into that conference room, faced a team of hulking, deadly, spec ops guys and never flinched. From that moment, she'd locked on to his confidence.

And now, the man who clearly had no issues being surrounded by other exceptional men was asking her to trust his judgment. Concerning Michael's pregnant wife. She slapped her hands on top of her head. "I know your instincts are great. This is personal though. Too much emotion involved."

"But in this case, the emotion is the key. He's a loving father holding a woman hostage. He will not want his son remembering this about him."

He leaned forward, pressed a kiss on her lips. "Trust me. Please?"

She kissed him back, let the sensation of its softness ease her panic for a few seconds. She hated being caught between supporting him and terror. Her heart banged inside her chest and she thought about Roxann and her unborn baby. It all came down to getting Roxann out of this and if Gavin thought he could do it, well, she'd have to believe in him. What harm could it do?

Aside from him getting killed.

· · ·

GAVIN PULLED BACK FROM THE KISS AND RESTED HIS HANDS ON her soft, cupid cheeks. "What do you say?"

"I say I hate you."

Not that he believed it with the smile she wore. For a few seconds he'd convinced himself she wouldn't agree with him. He wasn't sure when it happened, but her support had become vital to him. Here they were, two people in the chasm of coworkers becoming lovers. "Good," he said. "The mother will be here with the kid in thirty minutes."

"And then what?"

"Then I show Joe his son. First, I need to get him on the phone and convince him to meet face-to-face."

He snatched the headset and pressed the button. "Joe, it's getting late. I'm taking a walk over there and we'll talk face-to-face."

Only give him the options you want him to choose from. Another negotiator truth. And right now, there was only one choice Gavin wanted him to have.

"No."

"Joe, listen to me. My guys aren't going to move unless I give the word. Haven't I played straight with you all day?"

"Well, yeah, but how do I know you're not sending your army in?"

"Not gonna happen. Not with me in there with you. You know I want you to get out of there safely. I think we can talk this out and make that happen. Everyone can get what they need, Joe."

Need. Not want. Jackson Spelling wouldn't be getting out of jail. Not this way. Maybe Gavin was skirting the lie—*the only lie will be the last*—but this was as good a reason as any.

"Okay," Joe said. "Just you. And we search you before you come in."

Gavin pumped his fist. *Yes.* "Deal. My guys will line up

just like they did with the food, okay? Just like last time. Nothing crazy."

"No one comes near the house but you. We'll be watching all sides."

"Right. No problem. I'm on my way."

He punched the button and dropped the headset. Janet tore her headset off and bolted from her chair. "The son isn't here yet."

That was a small issue, but he'd do a work-around. "The sooner I get in there, the sooner Roxann comes out. Once I'm in, you radio me when the son gets here. We'll put the son in the driveway where he can see him."

"No."

Sorry, babe. "Yes." He marched to the table where he'd dropped his tac vest and slid it on.

Her hands went in the air. "Wait. Just hang on a second. Please."

"Why?"

"I can't think. *That's* why. This is not the plan you gave me. You told me you'd wait for the son and they wouldn't shoot with him around. Now you're saying you're going alone. It's too half-cocked."

A scalding stab of disappointment plunged into him.

Half. Cocked.

Gavin backed up a step, folded his arms because all damn day he'd been battling. Joe, Vic, the tactical guys. All of them at one point or another had been a pain in the ass. Not her. *She'd* been battling alongside him, replenishing his reserves, helping him figure it all out. And she chose now to bail on him?

Half. Cocked.

He breathed in, stared down at the woman who, in one day, claimed his heart and then broken it. He had no time for this *fucking* emotional vacuum forcing him to second-guess his decisions. His worst nightmare would be to walk into that house with his head a raging mess. Perfect way to get a hostage killed. He blew out a long breath and closed his eyes to center himself. *Get it together.*

A minute later he opened his eyes, stared down at Janet who fiddled with a rubber band, twisting it this way and that, working the kinks out. As if it were that easy. Not this time. He couldn't worry about it now. Now, he had to forget this emotional crap and get Roxann Taylor and her unborn child out of that house. Carefully, he fastened the tac vest and checked the strap. "I have to go."

He spun and marched out of the barn.

"Gavin!" Janet yelled, but he had already gotten halfway to the road while she scrambled to keep pace.

Forget the emotional crap. Think about the assignment.

"Janet, get back inside."

"Damn you!" she hollered. "You're testing me to see how far I'll take this."

A slippery slope right here. She'd been his partner, his ally, his supporter when the goddamned knuckle-dragger wanted to take over this operation. He did *not* need her doubting him. Not when he was about to walk into a situation that might get his head blown off. At this moment, she might not be grasping that though and he didn't have time to explain it.

Later.

"I'm not testing you. I need you to let me do my job so no one gets hurt."

That stopped her, but he kept walking, needing to put space between them and the swirling negative energy.

"Thank you," he called over his shoulder. "Call me on the radio when the son gets here." He held the radio to his mouth. "Jessup, I need you at the end of the driveway as you were before."

He glanced a hundred feet ahead of him, where Vic's team, suited up in their combat gear, moved from various places into position at the end of the driveway where the giant SUV pulled up. Still tromping up the road, Gavin took a breath of the warm air and looked beyond the men to the setting sun that streaked the sky in a burst of burnt orange. Without the heat, the chirping birds and swaying trees would make this a fine evening. Instead, he was trying to bring a pregnant woman home to her husband.

Gavin approached Jessup, who stood in front of him holding an MP5 9mm submachine gun. "Gavin, what's up?"

"I'm going in there."

Jessup threw the shield of his helmet up. "Come again?"

"I've got this guy's son on the way. I'm going in to talk him down. If it doesn't work, you boys can have at him."

Billy Tripp and one of the other guys, Bobby, straightened up, clearly not happy with the "have at him" comment.

"Does Vic know about this?"

"He will when he gets here."

Billy Tripp snorted. "This should be good."

"Shut it." Jessup turned back to Gavin. "What do you need?"

No argument. Finally. "Look like badasses and cover me."

Jessup lowered his shield again. "We can do that."

The three men lined up behind the SUV and Gavin heard Jessup murmur something into his radio, putting the rest of the team on alert.

Gavin marched up the driveway, his pulse raging, pounding under his skin, making him nauseous, but he concentrated on deep breaths. In and out. Step. Breath. Step. Breath. Step. Breath.

Halfway up the drive, he raised his arms. *Keep walking.* In two minutes he'd be inside. If he could get an ounce of luck, Joe's son wouldn't be far behind and they'd wrap this up quick. He stepped onto the sagging wooden porch—it would be a pisser if he fell through—and the front door inched open.

A blond guy, late twenties, khaki pants and a collared shirt stood in the tiny crack of the doorway. "Joe? I'm Gavin."

Joe nodded. "I recognize your voice."

Then he backed out of sight and pushed the door open.

I'm in.

5

———

Janet sat on her folding chair staring at the monitor as Gavin stepped into the house.

"Well, just damn him."

She should have been stubborn and kept walking with him. Even with the battle of wills, she might have been able to talk him out of this. Instead, he'd thrown himself into a situation that he might not come out of.

Slapping at the monitor, she said, "Damn you."

A car door from outside slammed—*terrific*—and she closed her eyes.

Barely through the door, Vic jabbed a finger at her. "What. The. *Fuck?*"

The fierce hardness in his eyes, all that anger barreling into her, set her back for a second and she breathed deep. *Don't panic.* She stood to her full five feet—*I'm small but I'm mighty*—and shoved her hands in front of her. "What's done is done."

"And what? You never heard of a goddamned phone?"

"As if I had time to call you while Gavin was marching up the road?"

"I should have been consulted. *Mike* should have been consulted."

She couldn't disagree. "There was no time. If you'll stop screaming at me, I'll update you. Where's Michael?"

"I left him up the road. Waiting for his wife. She'd better walk out."

In the few years Janet had worked for Vic, she'd seen every range of his emotions and this one was no exception. He was worried. Extremely so. Trying to calm him would be futile, but she never did shy away from a challenge.

"We found the HT's ex-girlfriend and she's on her way here with their son. Gavin thinks he can use the son as leverage."

"He put himself in danger by walking into that house unarmed."

Janet jerked her head. "He did."

"Fucking imbecile head-shrinker."

"He wants Roxann to get out safely."

He waved his arms. "And I don't?"

"I didn't say that. I know you do. You love her. We all love her. Gavin is close to getting this guy to break. He thinks by meeting face-to-face he can end it."

"And what if it doesn't work? Then he's a hostage with Rox."

A definite possibility. "I don't think that will happen. If this idea with the son doesn't work, he knows you'll breach."

"Damn straight. We're ready to go. All tuned up."

"Give him a little while. He can do this. Please?"

Come on, boss.

Vic dropped his hands to his hips. "When will the son be here?"

"In the next twenty minutes."

Come on, boss.

"Does head-shrinker have a radio?"

Janet didn't dare smile. "He does. He said to feel free to yell at him through it."

"I might do that."

"I told him we'd alert him when the son got here."

Stepping over to the desk, Vic stared at the monitor showing the front of the house. "From the minute that kid shows up, Gavin has twenty minutes. Then we're going in. No arguments. Tell him that." He marched toward the door. "I gotta give Mike an update."

An update. Hopefully the last one. Janet dropped into her chair, her shoulders sagging with the weight of simply holding her head high. So tired. She stared at the monitor above and sighed. "Gavin, you'd better be talking fast."

GAVIN STEPPED THROUGH THE FRONT DOOR WHERE JOE huddled behind it, a .38 in hand. One weapon accounted for. He did a visual survey of uncarpeted wood stairs leading to the second floor. To his right was the small living room with a worn three-cushioned sofa and two upholstered wing-back chairs. A solid brass lamp—possible weapon—sat on an ancient side-table with curling legs.

To his left, a doorway led to another room. He spotted the back of a chair and assumed the space was the dining room. Kitchen must be in the back.

Two men stood near the door leading to the dining room. The big one held a shotgun, and the smaller one, maybe mid-forties, wore jeans and a stained T-shirt. Gavin couldn't see a weapon on the smaller one. Didn't mean anything though.

Joe insisted on patting Gavin down and if it made them feel more comfortable, why not? He endured the search, keeping his mouth closed and his stance neutral. Why ignite the situation when he wasn't carrying anyway?

Upon completion of the search, Gavin refastened his tac vest.

"Joe, I need to make sure Mrs. Taylor is okay."

"She's fine. You don't need to see her."

Gavin cut his eyes to the grunts by the door. *Yes, I'm aware of you.* "Actually, I do. Then I can radio my people and tell them all is well. Where is she?"

After a ten-second hard stare—Joe's useless attempt at posturing—he caved. "Bring her down here. I don't want him going upstairs."

Even better. The closer Roxann got to the door, the faster he got her out of here. And where the hell was the son?

Jeans-Grunt spun from the doorway and headed toward the back of the house. *A second set of stairs?* Gavin, bent on controlling the environment despite that shotgun, gestured to the chairs. "Let's sit."

With slow, deliberate movements, he sat on the sofa and Joe dropped onto one of the chairs. "Where are we on Mr. Spelling's release? I'm tired of waiting."

Let the only lie be the last. "My boss has a call in to the governor. We're working on it."

One helluva lie because Mike hadn't made any such call. If he had, the FBI would be swarming this place. The lie, at this point, didn't matter. If he didn't talk these people out of here, a breach was imminent. That was the deal.

And Gavin would live with it. He'd go down talking though.

The soft tap of shoes on hardwood sounded and Roxann walked through the doorway, her eyes red and puffy and her shorts wrinkled, but her blond hair was tied back and neat. The woman knew how to pull off composure. No doubt.

She's unharmed.

He glanced at her sandaled feet. Flats. If they needed to run, heels wouldn't be an issue.

Despite the parade going on in his head, Gavin forced himself not to react. Out of habit, he moved to stand, but froze when Shotgun-Guy snapped to. Gavin held his hands out. "Take it easy. I'm just standing."

He rose, shoulders back, posture erect, making sure these guys knew he didn't fear them. Plus, his small act of rebellion allowed him to assert control. How he thrived on psychological warfare.

He did release a silent breath when Shotgun-Guy lowered his weapon.

"Rox, you okay?"

She cut her eyes to Jeans-Grunt. "I'm fine."

Gavin nodded. "Good." He turned to Joe. "I'd like her to have a seat down here. She's been locked up all day. Give her a break."

After a moment, Joe glanced at his cohorts. Shotgun-Guy gave an almost nonexistent shake of his head.

Power struggle.

Joe motioned Rox to the other end of the sofa, away from Gavin. "Sit there."

Success. Not only did Gavin win that round, he'd created a power play between Joe and Shotgun-Guy. Each victory got him closer to Roxann walking out of here.

They both took their places on the sofa. His radio crackled and he lowered the volume, lifting it to his ear. "Cargo has arrived," Jessup said.

Cargo. The son. Now they were getting somewhere.

Joe leaned forward. "What cargo?"

"Put him on," Gavin said into the radio.

Keeping his focus on Joe, Gavin handed him the radio. "We talked about your son and how much you love him."

And then Joe's eyes bugged out—*wham*—instant panic. *Control him.*

"Sit tight. He's fine. He's outside and wants to talk to you."

Joe swung his head left and right. "I don't believe you. It's a trick."

"No trick. He's in the barn. Knowing how much you love him, I thought if you talked to him, maybe we could end this standoff and everyone goes home. Okay? That sounds good, right?"

Agree with me. Go ahead.

He glanced at his cohorts and Shotgun-Guy once again shook his head no.

Counter attack. "We can bring your son out front if you want to see him."

Realization must have hit that his beloved child had been brought to this disaster and Joe slammed his hands against his head. "You sons of bitches brought my *son* here?"

"Not alone. His mother is with him."

The look on his face, that open-mouthed gawk, changed from dismay to mind-numbing horror in a split second, and Gavin wondered if he should have stuck to the playbook.

Joe shook his head. "Her too? Jesus."

"I know you love your son, Joe. Make this right for him. Do you want me to get him out front?"

"No! I'll talk to him on the radio."

Gavin lifted the radio, drew a calming breath to ease his rapidly rising pulse. *No turning back now.* All he could hope was that he hadn't royally screwed up by involving the kid. "Put Jason on."

A long minute later, he heard Janet's voice, not directly in the radio but as if talking to someone else and just the sound, that soft whispering, made him more determined to get Roxann home.

"He's here," Janet said. "Just push the button, buddy. Got it?"

Then came a pause. "Dad?"

Joe held the radio near his face, his finger tapping the side. He closed his eyes and gritted his teeth before dropping his hands.

Atta boy. Think about how you'll lay waste to this kid's life by dying in here.

After a minute, he lifted the radio again. "Hi, pal. Where are you?"

"With Mom in this barn, but it's not really a barn. There's all this cool stuff. Computers and monitors and walkie-talkies. There's a phone in a box! The lady said I could play with the phone. Can I come see you?"

Textbook. Gavin ignored the surge of adrenaline nearly blowing his skull apart. The third HT left the room and Gavin kept an eye on him from his spot.

"Not yet, pal," Joe said to his son. "In a little while. Okay?"

"Sure. Can you take me for ice cream like usual?"

Joe slammed his free hand against his forehead, did it once more, then marched to the front window and peeked out the blinds.

Think. About. It.

"Yeah, buddy. Ice cream it is. I gotta go now." He stopped, cleared his shattering voice. "I'll call you back soon."

He tossed the radio the few feet to the coffee table and it clattered against the cheap wood. *Don't give him time to think.*

"Joe, that's what you're risking. Ice cream with your son

every night. Is Jackson Spelling worth it? Maybe he is, I don't know, but from my perspective as a guy who lost his father at a young age, if something happens to you, your son won't recover. Make this right, Joe. Let me walk out of here with Roxann and we'll find another way to help you win the Jackson Spelling fight."

"No!" Shotgun-Guy yelled, swinging the barrel up.

"Hey!" Joe yelled back. "Calm down. If that thing goes off, you'll screw this whole thing up."

"Yeah, Joe, he will. You don't want that. Nobody gets hurt and we all go home to our families tonight. No harm, no foul."

But this scenario was turning to shit. Damned fast. Without a weapon, Gavin's options were few and Shotgun-Guy's unpredictability would hinder negotiations. Mentally, Gavin gauged the distance to Shotgun-Guy at fifteen feet. A charging man could cover twenty-one feet in one second or less.

One second of distraction.

That was all he needed to reach Shotgun-Guy. Except, Gavin was seated, not standing. He'd have to risk it.

"Lower that weapon!" Joe hollered and Shotgun-Guy took his eyes from Gavin to Joe.

Now.

Gavin exploded off the couch, taking the seat cushion with him and hurling it at Shotgun-Guy. It wouldn't do much, but it would absorb the impact of a bullet. A boom sounded and the shot tore through the cushion, pellets slamming into the Kevlar like tiny missiles. The vest kept the bullet from penetrating his right shoulder but the force knocked him back two steps. His breath caught at the raging pain ripping through his shoulder and chest. He glanced down, saw the outer portion of the vest shredded and knew he'd probably been hit with double-aught buck.

Son of a bitch.

"Gavin!" Roxann yelled and he swung his gaze to her, holding up his hand to keep her seated and out of the line of fire.

Get the gun.

Before Shotgun-Guy could get off another shot, Gavin charged. Grabbing the barrel with both hands, he wrenched it upward and, throwing all his weight into it, slowly forced the man backward. Gavin's arms burned, his muscles straining until Shotgun-Guy reached his spine's bending limit and dropped to the floor. Finally, he planted his foot on his chest, twisted the gun hard and jerked it free.

Got it.

With the gun pointed at Shotgun-Guy, he lifted his foot. "Flip over." Gavin waited for him to roll then jammed his foot into his back to hold him down. "Keep still."

At the front window, Joe stood with his gun aimed at Gavin. The tremble of his hand indicated fear. *Afraid to fire.*

"What the hell?" the third hostage taker hollered, charging in from the dining room.

"Don't move!" Gavin said and the guy halted. "Go over by Joe. On the floor, facedown, hands on your head. Now!"

In Gavin's mind, this guy's decision should not have been a difficult one. Considering the shotgun at his buddy's head. With assessing eyes, the guy swung his head to Joe, back to Gavin and that shotgun and hustled to the window where he dropped to the floor. In the sudden silence, voices —tight in their urgency—came over the radio. They'd have to wait a sec.

"Rox, you okay?"

"I am."

Joe swung his gun between Gavin and Roxann. "Nobody move!"

"Here's the deal," Gavin said. "I got a bunch of guys out there hoping to tear this place apart. We've just had shots fired. If I don't get on that radio and tell them something, they'll go balls to the wall. You don't want that. Rox, get on the radio and tell them we're okay."

Slowly, Roxann reached for the radio still on the coffee table.

"Thank you," he said. "When you're done, stay on the couch."

Away from the guns.

"Shots fired!" Janet yelled; her eyes focused on the monitor overhead.

Vic lifted his handset. "What are those goddamned shots? Status!"

"Inside the house," Monk said.

A small squeak sounded in Janet's throat. All day she'd kept the fear at bay, locked down that emotional swamp waiting to submerge her, to steal the air from her body, and now, just maybe, it would overtake her. "What if..."

Vic stared at her for a split second. "Focus!"

"We're fine." Roxann. Through the radio.

Janet's heart crumbled. Just fell apart in a way that left her body splintered and aching. Too much stress. She concentrated on staying alert as her breaths came fast and short. *God, Janet, don't cry.*

"No one is hurt." This from Gavin, but his voice sounded distant. As if away from the radio. "I've secured two of the HTs. Now Joe and I are gonna talk and see if we can resolve this."

"My ass," Vic said. "We're done here. My guys are coming in."

"Joe still has a weapon. Give me a few minutes."

"Crap," Janet muttered. She turned to her boss who stared at the ceiling, his head slowly moving back and forth. Contemplating. There were times when Vic was dug in. Resolute. During those times, his commands were swift and decisive. This was not one of those times.

"He can do this," she said. "He's already subdued two of them. He's been working this guy all day. Joe, on a certain level, trusts him. Give him ten more minutes."

A long moment passed where the only sounds registering were the whirring of her laptop and the rustle of leaves outside. Janet breathed in and her head stopped pounding. The fear had backed off. The emotional flood receding. *Thank you.*

Vic hit the button on his radio. "Ten minutes and we're coming in."

Gavin stared right into Joe's eyes. "You heard him. We've got ten minutes. We're either gonna kill each other or we'll walk out of here. What's it gonna be?"

Joe's gaze went to the HT wiggling around under Gavin's foot, the shotgun still pointed at him. The other guy stayed on the floor, but his eyes shifted back and forth. Roxann, being Roxann, twisted around, yanked the lamp cord from the wall, wrapped her hand around the heavy brass base and brought the lamp to her lap.

She understood the benefits of brass lamps as weapons. One good swing and she'd crack someone's skull.

"Hey!" Joe yelled, aiming the gun at her.

Gavin swung the shotgun in Joe's direction. "Relax. She's not going anywhere."

Rox removed the shade and checked the heft of the lamp. "Insurance."

No wonder Mike adored her. Right now though, he had eight minutes to get Joe's gun pointed back at him and end this thing.

"Joe, your mission is coming apart. Stop now and everyone walks out safely. Nobody is hurt. Nobody is dead."

From under Gavin's foot the guy on the floor said, "Don't—"

Gavin pressed his foot down. "You shut up."

After a gasping noise from his prisoner, figuring the point had been made, Gavin eased up. Joe's gaze bounced all over the room. Silent panic.

Move in.

"Somehow," Gavin said, "whoever these guys are, whatever they mean to you, I don't think they rank with watching your son grow into a man. That's the only decision you need to make right now. Are these two, this *mission,* worth you losing the opportunity to take your son for ice cream every night? Or to ballgames for the next twenty years? Watching him graduate? Get married? What's it worth to you, Joe?"

With any luck, it would be enough to get them out of there.

Janet sat on the stupid, miserable, spine-mangling folding chair, her equally miserable boss towering over her, his gaze glued to the monitor above her head, both of them —for different reasons—counting down the minutes. Theoretically, she and Vic were of the same mind in wanting the standoff to be over, but Vic wanted to breach and Janet wanted everyone to exit on their own.

Either way, she supposed, someone could die. And maybe she was a horrible person, but she didn't want either person to be Gavin or Roxann. The other ones? They created this mess; they'd have to deal with the consequences.

Horrible person.

"Five minutes," Vic announced.

He strode to the table and grabbed a vest, sliding it on with the ease of a man putting on a dress shirt. "I'm heading up there. Mike is probably ready to haul ass into the house. Without a vest or weapon. Goddamned head-shrinker."

Enough already. Beleaguered from the battle of controlling her emotions, her last standing nerve snapped. She shot out of her chair. "He was afraid Rox would get hurt. That's why he went in. He's trying to save her and you being a pain in the butt is not helping."

But Vic was already out the door. Not that he would have listened anyway. At least not in his current mental state. Another thing she knew about her boss. When he was in his zone—as in now—he only dealt with the task at hand.

Jason's mother entered the barn, her face drawn. Jason didn't trail behind and Janet assumed he would still be in his mother's car. "What's happening?"

"I'm not sure." *Liar.* "Give me a couple of minutes to find out. Please, go back to your car and wait. Just until we know what's going on."

"Is he dead? Joe?"

And, oh, God, she needed some better people skills. What was she supposed to say to this woman whose son might wind up fatherless? *Totally inept at this.* Lacking options, she'd go with the truth. At least what she knew to be the truth. "No."

The woman dropped her chin to her chest. "He's a good father. Maybe he's mixed up, but he adores Jason."

Janet squeezed her arm. "I know. I was listening while he and Gavin talked. We're trying to get him out safely. If you'll promise to stay in your car, I'll see if I can get you information. Will you do that for me?"

"Please, hurry."

Janet grabbed a radio, spotted Gavin's iPod and snatched that, as well. He'd want it when he came out. Yes, she'd allow herself to believe it. Allow the words to convince her that he would indeed walk out.

JOE LOWERED HIS GUN AND GAVIN'S HEAD THROBBED.

Not home yet.

"No!" Shotgun-Guy yelled.

When it came to the idiot under his foot, Gavin's insistence on a nonviolent resolution quickly dissolved. He leaned in, adding extra pressure this time. "You shut up."

His gaze solid on Shotgun-Guy, Joe said, "I'm done. I have a son to think about."

"Pussy!"

This dumbass wouldn't shut the hell up. Gavin leaned in harder. "Are you gonna keep quiet or do I have to shoot you?"

Shotgun-Guy bobbed his head. Finally. Gavin eased up, then swung his gun back to Joe. "I need you to put the gun on the floor and kick it toward the door."

Half a second later, his shoulders stooped, Joe set the gun on the battered wood floor and slid it away.

"Good. Now, on the floor. Hands on top of your head."

Joe did as he was told. "Rox, come around this way and grab that gun. Please."

Not until Gavin had that weapon secured and Roxann out of this hellish place would he be relieved. A surrender could disintegrate in a thousand different ways. A thousand different ways that included dead hostage takers, dead hostages and dead negotiators.

None of which appealed.

BY THE TIME JANET GOT TO THE ROAD, VIC HAD MICHAEL wedged behind the cover of a tree. Another conversation she'd be totally inept at.

She concentrated on the house and the quiet country air. The rustle of leaves. Chirping birds.

All pleasant sounds that didn't include gunshots.

Maybe they'd get out of this. She held the radio to her lips. "Gavin? What's happening?"

Silence.

Dammit. He'd better not die, that's all she had to say. But that fierce, nagging panic seized her and her stomach pitched and rolled and rolled again. She didn't want to imagine his body riddled with bullet holes, blood seeping, stealing the life from him.

She picked up her pace, walked by the tree toward the driveway.

"Hey!" Vic yelled. "Where the hell are you going?"

She kept walking.

"Well, goddammit," Vic said and suddenly she was yanked backward, stumbling against her boss.

Janet blinked a couple of times, zoomed in on the taut features of his face. *Mad face.*

"I need you to get it together," he said. "You've got no vest on, no helmet and you're about to walk into a hot zone. I don't have time for you to get nuts on me. Got it?"

But I think I love him.

There it was, the admission to herself. The risking her life because a simple crush had grown into a deep yearning. Emotionally, she'd known it after that first kiss three weeks ago. Intellectually, she didn't want to admit it.

Vic snapped his fingers in front of her face. "You in there?"

She nodded. "I've got it. Sorry."

And then her radio crackled. *Thank God.* "We're coming out," Gavin said. "Send the men in to secure the HTs."

Various sounds and colors exploded in her head. The chaos breaking free. Her body sagged with relief—or maybe it was simply exhaustion.

What a damned day.

Michael lurched away from the tree, but Vic rammed a hand into his chest. "Wait. Let's get it cleared."

Monk led the team into the house and seconds later the front door opened. Roxann stepped onto the porch with Gavin on her heels. Movement from the right drew Janet's attention. Michael shoved Vic and sprinted down the driveway.

Wow. Who knew the boss could run like that?

"Mike!" Vic yelled.

Janet grabbed Vic's arm. "Let him go."

I know how he feels. Gavin ushered Roxann down the porch stairs and she held her arms open for her charging husband, who nearly knocked her backward. They held on for a long minute, just the two of them in that blasted drive-way, clinging to each other, offering shelter from this horrid, horrid day.

Wow.

Without warning, the vile sadness Janet had buried in the deepest part of her tunneled its way out, clawing at her, reminding her she was a lonely computer geek who had long been misunderstood by the world. And worse, she was a lonely computer geek coveting the love Roxann Taylor had.

God's sake, Janet, the woman was held hostage.

Sparing not a glance at Michael and Roxann, Gavin walked by them and headed straight toward her. She breathed in. Could this be the man who would finally accept, without judgment, her need to spend hours in front of a computer? The one strong enough to withstand the ridiculous amount of testosterone surrounding her on a daily basis?

On cue, a huge chunk of that testosterone, namely Vic, marched down the driveway toward Gavin, and Janet half ran to keep on his heels. Too damned many long-legged people in this world.

The three of them met halfway down the drive and Gavin stared at her for three seconds—she'd counted—before addressing Vic. "Everyone is safe. Your team is securing the HTs and the weapons."

She spotted the tattered material on Gavin's tac vest and sucked in a breath. "You got shot?"

"No. My vest got shot."

Funny man. She'd slap him later. "Are you hurt?"

He slid his gaze to her. "No. The vest did its job."

By the looks of that vest, it must have been a wallop.

Vic glanced to the house and shook his head. "Jesus, head-shrinker. You got a set of stones. Freaking lunatic."

"Rudeness!" Janet said.

Gavin laughed. "Yeah, well, this mess is your problem now. You and Mike need to get Rox in front of a judge with these dopes. She'll present probable cause in relation to the abduction and these boys are off the streets."

"You know it, head-shrinker. They're going down on this one. I'll take them to the PD myself."

Roxann would receive justice for her ordeal, but Joe's son would lose his father. No winners anywhere and Janet's heart tore an inch for that sweet young boy. At least his father was alive. She'd never understand how a man allowed himself to get sucked into something that risked his child's happiness.

No wonder she spent so much time avoiding people.

Her gaze moved back to Michael and Roxann, still in the driveway, with Michael smothering kisses over her face and hands and then—would you look at that—her belly. After this, he'd never let Rox go anywhere alone. What a battle that would be. And so fun to watch. The insidious envy from moments ago vanished and Janet closed her eyes.

She'd get her turn.

She would.

She'd just have to wait.

The sound of the front door slapping alerted Vic to his team exiting the house and he marched toward them. Janet remained mesmerized by Michael and Roxann. "Did you see that?" she asked Gavin. "Amazing."

When he didn't respond, she retrieved the iPod from her pocket and held it out. He focused on her outstretched hand, but stayed quiet. Was having the iPod pushing it? Somehow an invasion? Too familiar? What?

People.

Give her a computer any day.

"It's not a big deal," she said. "I thought you might want it."

He scooped the iPod from her hand and grabbed her

arm. "Come with me. We'll talk to the mother and son and send them on their way."

That was it? Minutes ago, she'd admitted to herself that she loved this man and he was back to business as usual? Really? That bit about him being the one who might understand her?

Forget it.

GAVIN TALKED VIC INTO LETTING JOE SAY GOODBYE TO HIS son. The guy might be a certified nut job, but his son deserved a few minutes with the father he'd spend years without.

At least the kid would be able to visit a prison instead of a cemetery.

Something to be thankful for.

Watching the kid hug his father opened an enormous, aching hole in Gavin's chest and he turned away.

"You okay?" Janet asked.

Maybe. If he could fill the hole, yes, he'd be okay. Once again, he grabbed Janet's arm, hauling her with him to the barn. When he'd walked out of that house with Roxann, the sight of Janet holding his iPod sent every emotion he possessed on a high-speed chase. She hadn't just handed him the device; she understood his need to go inside himself and unwind. To relieve the stress and center himself.

Not only that, she *encouraged* it. How rare had it been to find a woman who had no expectation that he'd immediately talk about his feelings? Most times he *never* talked about his feelings. And women, at least the ones who had entered his realm, took issue with that.

But here stood quirky, dedicated Janet Fink who might

be the person to fill that hollow place in his chest. If so, he'd have to step up and let her know.

Once inside the barn, he pulled the door closed and walked right up to her, his gaze steady on hers. *Step up.* "Yes. I saw that. Mike and Roxann. Yes, it was amazing."

For years now he'd put his life on the line, trading places with hostages and jumping into mental battle with lunatics. Sure he'd saved lives, but at what cost? He'd lost a marriage to his job, not to mention a chunk of his own emotional freedom. If he continued on this path, in a few short years he'd be burned-out human flesh.

Not exactly something worth attaining. Beyond that, all he knew was Janet had been the first person he'd seen when he stepped out of the house.

She was important. What she'd be in his life, he wasn't sure, but he knew he wanted to experience it.

Step up.

He kissed her. A solid press of his lips as he gathered this tiny peanut of a woman into his arms, crushing her ribs, wanting to feel her heartbeat. Everyone was alive. *He* was alive. After facing a shotgun aimed at him, he'd figured out what was important.

Resisting the urge to strip her naked in this broken-down barn, he backed away from the kiss. "Here it is." She blinked a couple of times, focused those big brown eyes on him and he decided he might just be driven to begging. "You don't report to me. I'm in no way your superior. You report to Vic."

"Exactly."

He squeezed her arms. "Can you deal with the gossip? Because it'll be raging."

"I know. It scares the hell out of me."

"Me too. But the gossip will die down and then it'll be us

figuring each other out. That's what I want. I want to figure out my life with you in it. I think *that* will be amazing."

Not a peep out of her. She stood there, her mouth partly open, her gaze leaving skid marks on his face.

He held his hands out. "What are you thinking?"

"That I've successfully turned stupid and it's not so bad."

He laughed.

"It's not funny. Not for a second. I've spent years trying to be the unslut. The girl people took seriously because of her skills. I've been brutal to myself. And then this thing with Rox happened and I'm questioning everything."

"Sometimes questioning is good. Is it good now?"

She hesitated, her eyes on his. "It *feels* good. Which scares me even more. I've always been the socially inept computer geek and you're, well, you could talk a cow into a vacation at a slaughterhouse. In some crazy way, we balance out. So, I'm gonna say screw it and live a little. The witch twins can kiss my ass."

Then she did that crazy monkeylike thing when she threw her arms around his neck, leaped up, wrapped her legs around his waist and kissed him. Funny woman and he couldn't help laughing, which turned out to be complicated. What with her *tongue* in his *mouth*.

A squeak came from the direction of the barn door. Someone coming in. *Jig's up.*

"Ack!" the knuckle-dragger hollered.

Gavin broke away from the kiss.

"Oops," Janet said.

"Get lost." Gavin jerked his head toward the door. "We can handle this."

But Vic already had his hands over his eyes. "Are you *shitting* me? Did I need to see that? I think I'm fucking blind!"

Janet grinned. "I told you his eyes would bleed."

He shrugged. "I guess he'll have to get used to it."

She twisted to look at Vic. "Hear that, boss? The head-shrinker says you'll have to get used to it. Go home to your family and leave us alone." She turned back to Gavin, her lips curving into a wicked smile. "We might be here a while."

Want more of the Private Protectors series? Read on to enjoy an excerpt from *A Just Deception*.

A JUST DECEPTION
BY ADRIENNE GIORDANO

Enjoy an excerpt from *A Just Deception*, book four in the
Private Protector Series:

Chapter One

From her crouched position filling the copy machine
drawer, Isabelle spied her cousin Kendrick in the doorway
and knew the next few minutes would be worse than a bad
case of chicken pox. Irritating as hell and no scratching

allowed. Already he blocked her only exit from the cramped room—that was no accident. She drew a searing breath and straightened to her full height, determined to confront him.

Kendrick wore black chinos and a white Oxford shirt, but the preppy clothes couldn't hide the predator. With a shudder, she remembered everything about him she would rather forget. Despite her resolve, the small room pressed in, and she backed away.

Damn.

His leer forced her to dig her heels into the floor and a relentless gnawing tore at her stomach.

Lawyer mode. Now.

"Kendrick, it's been a while."

Three years, two months and thirteen days.

"I'm here to see my father," he said. "I saw you in here. Thought I'd say hello."

She leaned against the copy machine, folded her arms and squeezed until her fingernails bit into her biceps. After years spent grappling to rise above her brokenness, something in his tone—that confident, you'll-never-get-me attitude—shattered her. "Well, I'm sure your father is waiting for you."

"I'm a few minutes early."

"Your father prides himself on the comfortable waiting area. Maybe you can find something to read while you wait."

Kendrick ignored her suggestion and moved into the compact room. She remained still, but tracked him with her eyes, watching him until he halted a foot from her. *Too close.*

A quick glance across his shoulder revealed the safety of the outer corridor where two associates spoke in hushed voices. Assistance was nearby if needed, but screaming for help against the boss's son? How humiliating. Not to mention having to explain it. "I have a client in my office."

He inched closer, and Isabelle held up a hand to stop him. Silly her for believing he would let her leave. She had to get away.

"I need to talk to you," he said.

Okay. Deep breath. She concentrated on diffusing the internal bedlam this man caused. *Get a grip. Don't give him the control. Don't look at him.*

After a few seconds, her thundering pulse settled to its normal rhythm. She could do this.

"I'm in the middle of a client meeting." She turned, made the copy she'd come in for, grabbed her papers and attempted to push by him.

Kendrick sidestepped to block her exit. Unbelievable. She was trapped in here with him. Close enough to feel his breath on her skin.

"I only need a couple of minutes, Isabelle."

Never. He didn't deserve it. Not after what he'd taken from her already.

She met his gaze straight on, their eyes locking for an instant. "I don't have time, Kendrick."

"I have an offer for you."

Any offer from him could result in her losing a slice of her soul. Her answer would certainly be no. She found triumph in that. Telling him no. Definitively.

She'd let him say what he needed to, indulge in saying no and then boot him out. "Two minutes."

"Oh, Isabelle. You do amuse me."

She made a show of checking her watch. "Now it's one minute."

"You know I've bought property in Ohio, correct?"

Oh, she knew. She was thankful every day that the state of Pennsylvania normally provided a barrier between them. Living on the Jersey Shore rewarded her with a sense of ease, and Kendrick being in the area chipped that comfort. "If you need legal advice, talk to someone else. I won't be objective."

He laughed, his big white teeth flashing. Isabelle ground the heel of her black pump into the floor. Her leg ached from the pressure, but the pain would keep her focused.

"*Anyway*," he said. "I'd like to have you visit. Take a look at the place. Maybe stay in one of the bungalows. It's a wonderful piece of property."

"No."

He held up his hands again. "I know you're still angry over the misunderstanding, but let's put it behind us. We're family. I *know* my father would appreciate you letting go of the hostility. Come see the compound. Stay awhile. You'll be taken care of. Any need or want you have will be fulfilled by one of the staff members."

What was all this babbling about his compound?

She narrowed her eyes and let his comment about his father—her boss—roll off her. Convincing herself to accept a job from Kendrick's father hadn't been easy, but working at one of New Jersey's top criminal defense firms would catapult her career. Her cousin's goading wouldn't jeopardize that. "I need to get back to work."

"Not staff, really," he continued. "Tenants, I guess. Fifty of us live on the property. Some in the main house and some in bungalows scattered throughout the hundred acres. You'd have your own place, of course."

A flicker of perverse excitement twinkled in his blue-green eyes, and sickness swirled in her stomach. She needed to get him out of there before the toxic waste he spewed consumed her.

"I'm not interested."

Kendrick reached down and tugged at the sleeves of his shirt, but made no move to leave. Idiot.

And yet, she remained wedged in the room. With a client waiting in her office. The brutal pressure of these few minutes finally overtook her, and a chill penetrated her bones, puckering her skin.

Don't let him win.

He tried the slick smile that always worked on the little girl she'd once been, and she imagined him bursting into flames.

"I need you, Isabelle. There are...things happening and I could use your legal expertise. I promise I'll take good care of you." He dragged his gaze over her body. "I always did."

Sick, sick, sick.

She fisted her free hand until her knuckles popped. Her only other choice would be to pummel him. Probably not a good idea in his father's building.

A knock on the doorframe brought deflating relief to her tense body. Her assistant stood there, her eyes shifting to Kendrick and back. "Mr. Parker is looking for you. I would have made the copies."

"You were away from your desk. Besides, we're done."

"I'll give you time to think about it," Kendrick said.

"Don't bother. My answer will still be no."

No. No. No.

After her meeting with Mr. Parker concluded, Isabelle dialed a familiar cell phone number. Vic Andrews, a long-time family friend, lived in Chicago, but he'd come through for her. He answered on the second ring.

"Ah, the lovely Isabelle DeRosa."

She sat back in her desk chair. The late afternoon sun blanketed her arm, and she shifted toward the window for the full effect. Between the sun and Vic's Southern charm, a comforting feeling enveloped her.

A long, piercing car horn sounded and Vic let out a stream of creative swearing. All righty, then.

"What's going on?" Vic asked after his verbal tirade ended.

"Where are you?"

"I'm attempting to pick up Lily from day camp. I gotta tell ya, Cambodian jungles are easier to get through than this line. I should put some of these moms on my staff. They'd be world-class operators."

Isabelle snorted. A former special ops guy, he'd seen a lot of action in his lifetime.

"What's up?" he asked.

She swallowed hard and fiddled with her pen. Vic was one of the few people outside the family that knew her secret. "Kendrick is back."

"Son of a bitch. Is it a permanent thing?"

"No. He wants me to visit him in Ohio."

Silence. She knew how he felt. Helpless and stunned.

Vic finally spoke. "What the fuck?"

"Exactly. He's as nuts as ever. He cornered me in the copy room at the office."

"Did you beat the crap out of him?"

"I wanted to," Isabelle said.

"What can I do?"

Kill him. Heaven help her. That would be all she needed. Thinking back on the years she'd lost and what Kendrick did to her, she probably did have that much anger. Scary.

She tossed her pen on the desk and picked a piece of lint from her slacks. "I need a security system on my house."

"Done," Vic said. "I'd rather hit him with a double pop

between the eyes, but if you want a security system, it's yours. I've been telling you that."

"Nag, nag, nag."

"You know it, darlin'. I've got a guy out there on vacation in Nosrum. I'll get him over to your place ASAP."

She had no doubt she could defend herself, but the alarm would be added protection. She knew damn well Kendrick wouldn't go away so easily.

Chapter Two

Peter stormed through the gates of his parents' estate with the roar of the Challenger's four hundred twenty-five horsepower engine sounding like heaven. He imagined the look on his mother's face and grinned. She despised loud cars. Particularly those driven by one of her sons. Another thing they didn't agree on. The cars he'd collected over the years were part of the draw of coming home to Jersey where he kept them stored in a climate-controlled garage built on his parents' property.

He pulled up the drive, but his mother's Cadillac was nowhere to be seen. He needed to stop and get his surfboard from the upstairs bedroom closet so at least he could say he'd been there. It would save him the lambasting she'd give him for not coming around enough. His father would be at work this time of day, and he made a mental note to call him. Dad at least gave him a break from the constant verbal pounding about living up to the Jessup name.

Peter stepped from the car, shielded his eyes against the blistering August sun, and scanned the three-story brick house—mansion really—he'd grown up in. Red, yellow and pink flowers dotted the front garden. He'd never once spied a weed on this property. His mother ran a tight ship.

He glanced at a four-foot potted tree to the right of the stone stairs, and a clanging erupted in his ears. Had the tree been there when he drove by yesterday? Definitely not. He'd have noticed it.

Possible hiding places no longer got by him. Not anymore. His blood pumped and his brain snapped until his nerves flew into overdrive. He fired a sideways kick at the tree and—bang—sent it barreling to its side.

Nothing there.

Shit.

He leaned forward, bracing his hands on his knees. Now he was seeing terrorists behind greenery? Vic was right. He was losing his mind.

Springsteen's "Born to Run" erupted from the pocket of his cargo shorts. He dug his phone out and checked the ID. Vic. The guy must be a mind reader.

"What's up?" Peter said, still eyeballing the toppled plant.

"You sound pissy. You got a bug up your ass?"

"Yeah. A six-foot-five one. Calling to check on my mental status?"

"Monk, don't be an asshole. Mike agreed with me. Most people would love their boss to give them an extended vacation."

Well, Peter—Monk, as the guys called him—wasn't most people. As a former Navy SEAL, he needed some kind of action at all times. When he walked into a room, everyone knew he was the alpha dog. The alpha dog didn't like being told he was on the verge of a breakdown. He considered it an insult.

Then again, he'd just kicked over a plant.

"This is a social call then? I'm fine, thanks, gotta go." He hung up, slid the phone back in his pocket and squatted to reset the plant.

The phone rang again, and he straightened to answer it.

Vic laughed in his ear. "Dickhead."

Peter grunted. Vic bullied his way around every damn thing. They'd worked together for three years now, since Peter joined Taylor Security after leaving the navy. The Chicago-based company handled residential and corporate security, and Vic's team did government contract work. When the government needed plausible deniability, they called Taylor Security. Everything from protection details for overseas diplomats to badass counter terrorism assignments—leveling chemical plants, destroying enemy caves, snatching a bad guy—that Peter thrived on. His last two assignments were the reason for this extended vacation.

Peter pinched the bridge of his nose. He didn't need this. "Can I call you back when I don't want to tear your head off and shove it up your ass?"

"I need a favor."

A *favor*? The guy had stones the size of Texas.

"You're kidding, right? Three days ago you called me into your office and told me to hand over my weapon and enjoy my family for a few extra weeks after my brother's wedding. It's gonna take me longer than three days to work that off. Call me back in a week. Maybe then I'll do your favor."

"I saved your life last summer," Vic shot back.

Dammit. Peter threw his head back and closed his eyes. "You only get to play that card once. Make it good."

ALSO BY ADRIENNE GIORDANO

PRIVATE PROTECTORS SERIES

Risking Trust

Man Law

Negotiating Point

A Just Deception

Relentless Pursuit

Opposing Forces

THE LUCIE RIZZO MYSTERY SERIES

Dog Collar Crime

Knocked Off

Limbo (novella)

Boosted

Whacked

Cooked

Incognito

The Lucie Rizzo Mystery Series Box Set 1

The Lucie Rizzo Mystery Series Box Set 2

The Lucie Rizzo Mystery Series Box Set 3

THE ROSE TRUDEAU MYSTERY SERIES

Into The Fire

HARLEQUIN INTRIGUES

The Prosecutor

The Defender

The Marshal

The Detective

The Rebel

JUSTIFIABLE CAUSE SERIES

The Chase

The Evasion

The Capture

CASINO FORTUNA SERIES

Deadly Odds

JUSTICE SERIES w/MISTY EVANS

Stealing Justice

Cheating Justice

Holiday Justice

Exposing Justice

Undercover Justice

Protecting Justice

Missing Justice

Defending Justice

SCHOCK SISTERS MYSTERY SERIES w/MISTY EVANS

1st Shock

2nd Strike

3rd Tango

STEELE RIDGE SERIES w/KELSEY BROWNING

A NOTE TO READERS

Dear reader,

Thank you for reading *Negotiating Point*. I hope you enjoyed it. If you did, please help others find it by sharing it with friends on social media and writing a review.

Sharing the book with your friends and leaving a review helps other readers decide to take the plunge into the world of the Private Protectors. I would appreciate it if you would consider taking a moment to tell your friends how much you enjoyed the story. Even a few words is a huge help. Thank you!

Happy reading!
Adrienne

ABOUT THE AUTHOR

Adrienne Giordano is a *USA Today* bestselling author of over thirty romantic suspense and mystery novels. She is a Jersey girl at heart, but now lives in the Midwest with her ultimate supporter of a husband, sports-obsessed son and Elliot, a snuggle-happy rescue. Having grown up near the ocean, Adrienne enjoys paddle-boarding, a nice float in a kayak and lounging on the beach with a good book.

For more information on Adrienne's books, please visit www.AdrienneGiordano.com.

Adrienne can also be found at:
Facebook.com/AdrienneGiordanoAuthor
Twitter.com/AdriennGiordano
Goodreads.com/AdrienneGiordano
Sign up for Adrienne's newsletter at:
https://adriennegiordano.com/newsletter